SILENCED

Simon Packham was born in Brighton. During his time as an actor he was a blind fiddler on HMS Bounty, a murderous vicar, a dodgy witness on *The Bill* and a variety of servants including Omar Sharif's personal footman and a coffin carrier for Dame Judi Dench.

He now writes fiction and lives in West Sussex with his wife, two children, a cat called Pax, and a number of hamsters.

comin 2 gt u was his first novel for children, and received great praise for its thrilling narrative, and exploration of cyber-bullying.

The Bex Factor hilariously questioned our fame obsessed society's love of reality TV.

Silenced is Simon's third book for Piccadilly Press.

Find out more at www.simonpackham.com and read an interview on www.piccadillypress.co.uk

SILENCED

SIMON PACKHAM

PICCADILLY PRESS • LONDON

For my first comedy partner, Big D

First published in Great Britain in 2012
by Piccadilly Press Ltd,
5 Castle Road, London NW1 8PR
www.piccadillypress.co.uk

A catalogue record for this book is available
from the British Library

ISBN: 978 1 84812 210 9 (paperback)
ISBN: 978 1 84812 211 6 (ebook)

Printed and bound by CPI Group (UK) Ltd, Croydon, CR0 4YY
Cover design by Nick Stearn
Cover photo © Getty

Teenager Killed in Car Accident

Facebook tributes are flooding in for St Thomas's Community College pupil Declan Norris, 15, who died in the early hours of Monday morning after the blue Ford Fiesta he was travelling in crashed into a tree.

His mother Hilary Norris, 45, described him as a 'fun loving teenager with a passion for all types of comedy and pepperoni pizza'.

The driver and three other passengers escaped with minor injuries.

Eight Months
After The Crash

If I tell you what happened, you've got to promise not to get all weird about it. What I did was totally dumb. Then again, *you* didn't exactly behave like a brain surgeon, did you, Declan? I mean, you were my best mate since, like, forever – the other half of the greatest comedy double-act never to play the Edinburgh Festival – but I still don't really understand why you got into that car.

Looking good by the way. Some saddo has laminated your picture and pinned it to the tree. It's that photo I took on the war graves trip, when old Catchpole was going on about the 'senseless waste of young life', and you couldn't stop laughing. You're fading a bit now, and underneath there's a terrible poem that rhymes *tragedy* with *KFC*, but at least you haven't erupted in über zits like I have in the last eight months, two weeks and four days.

I'm sorry I left it so long. I figured if the sun was shining it wouldn't be so bad. And if you ignore the decaying carpet of 'floral tributes' and that Arsenal scarf (which is a bit of a mystery because everyone knows you hated football), you could almost imagine that here, beneath a beech tree at the side of a winding country road, is the perfect place to snuff it. I know you once said that picturesque was just another word for rubbish, but believe it or not, I'm kind of into natural beauty these days, and you've got to admit, it's pretty mellow out here.

At least it would be if I could stop thinking about that assembly in Year Nine when three fire fighters lugged in a mangled car wreck and it grossed us out when we spotted real bloodstains. They said on the local news that you died in the arms of a paramedic. And I often wonder about your dying words. Knowing you, you probably cracked a joke. Which reminds me: did you realise that death is hereditary?

So what's the deal with the afterlife? Is it like time travel, where you're not allowed to intervene in history in case you upset the space/time continuum? Or can you slam doors and move cups and stuff? Because if you can, Declan, *why the hell didn't you warn me what I was getting into?* Maybe you were too busy hanging out with Charlie Chaplin and the other comedy legends. Or maybe . . . well . . . maybe there's no such thing as the afterlife and, like Mum and Dad, you just didn't have a clue what I was getting up to.

So let me park my bike against your tree and then, if you've got time, I'll bring you up to speed. What do you think of the helmet by the way? You won't believe this, but my mum's *even* more protective since you died. If she had her way, I wouldn't leave the house without full body armour. Thanks a lot, Declan.

Soz, that's not fair. She only gives me the cotton wool treatment because of what happened afterwards. According to a well-respected healthcare professional (and we're not talking the problem page woman in *The County Times* here), I have no reason to feel guilty. But whichever way you look at it, I must have been out of my mind.

We should have got a pizza in. If this is going to make any sense, I'll have to start at the beginning. Well, you're not going anywhere, are you?

The Morning After
After The Crash

'What's the matter, Chris?' said Luke Corcoran, who'd downloaded a hair-clipper sound effect and was running round our tutor base giving everyone short back and sides with his iPhone. 'Missing your boyfriend, are you?'

'Yeah, brilliant,' I said, wondering why we'd found him so terrifying until, round about the middle of Year Ten, he suddenly turned into a bit of a joke.

Rob 'The Slob' Adams was straightening his tie in the fold-up mirror he kept in his brown leather messenger bag. 'Declan's always late. He won't get very far in life if he doesn't start taking it more seriously.'

'What like you, you mean?' I said, jumping to your defence, even though I didn't particularly feel like it that morning. 'Declan would rather cut his head off and drown it in a bucket of his own vomit than be head boy.'

'It's head student actually,' said Rob the Slob. 'And you and your "hilarious" friend won't be laughing when you've got zilch all to write on your university application forms. It's only two years away, you know.'

I'd secretly fancied her since Year Seven, but Tash Wilson looked even hotter since they'd removed her brace. 'No wonder Dec's late,' she said. 'You should have seen him at Ella's party.'

'No one told me there was a party,' said Luke Corcoran, suddenly losing enthusiasm for his comedy hairdressing.

'What was Declan doing, anyway?' I said, trying to sound like I didn't give a monkey's.

Tash Wilson flashed her orthodontically remastered smile. 'The usual,' she said. 'Being funny. But you were there too, weren't you, Chris? You're his shadow, aren't you?'

It hurt even more when *she* said it. 'Look, I am *not* . . . I had to revise for the science assessment, that's all.'

'Oh well,' said Tash. 'He seemed to manage perfectly well without you.'

We'd always said that double-acts with a straight guy and a comic were dead old-fashioned, and it really got to me when people assumed that you were the only funny man.

Anyway, it was business as usual: Luke Corcoran was staking his claim to the Nobel Stupid Prize, Tash

Wilson was being unattainable, and you were late. So when Mr Lemon burst through the door and ripped off his beanie, it felt like every other Monday morning at St Thomas's Community College for the criminally insane.

'Oi, sir,' said Luke Corcoran. 'I like your hair.'

'Not now, Luke,' said Mr Lemon, his slaphead still glistening from the run to work. 'We need to get up to the sports hall asap. Mr Edmonds wants to talk to the whole school.'

'What about registration, sir?' said Rob the Slob.

'We haven't got time. You're all here, aren't you?'

'All except Declan Norris,' said Rob the Slob. 'He's late – as usual.'

'Been out partying, sir,' said Luke Corcoran, tapping the side of his nose. 'Know what I mean?'

Mr Lemon ran his hand through a thick mop of imaginary hair. 'Look, we really haven't got time to —'

'Don't run with the bums, mate. *Walk* with guys,' said Luke Corcoran. He couldn't do the Australian accent like you, but everyone laughed because it was one of your catchphrases.

'*Please,*' said Mr Lemon, who sounded all wrong when he begged. 'We need to get a move on.'

Eleven LV (minus one) trooped over to the sports hall with the same enthusiasm we reserved for fire drills.

'Why weren't the prefects told about this?' said Rob the Slob. 'It's a complete shambles.'

Everyone knew it was a waste of time. If you'd been there, we could have compared notes on the latest episode of *Family Guy*, but I didn't think I could stand another 'mindless vandalism' lecture.

And it looked like most of the teachers felt the same way. Come to think of it, they always look miserable on Monday mornings – and I'd seen Miss Hoolyhan crying after some of her school concerts.

The Demon Headmaster has two public faces: his hideous 'record GSCE results' smile and his drowning not waving death mask, which he wore now, and seemed to come more naturally. 'I'm afraid I have some very grave news for you all.'

I couldn't help letting out a stifled 'Ha'. Mr Edmonds's idea of grave news was that the girls' skirts had crept up half a millimetre.

'Late last night, a Year Eleven boy was involved in a serious car accident.'

Silence fell over the basketball courts as the beast that is St Thomas's Community College held its breath and waited for him to name names. But it didn't take record GCSE results to figure it out. Those joyriders off the Dogshit Estate were an accident waiting to happen.

'Tragically, while the rest of the passengers escaped unhurt, the St Thomas's pupil sustained serious head injuries and – despite the best efforts of the emergency services – passed away at the scene of the accident.'

The chances were I didn't even know him. It was probably some kid from the reluctant learners unit.

'Declan Norris was a valued member of the school community. In Year Seven he served with distinction on the school council. More recently, he took part in our highly successful production of *Little Shop of Horrors*, as well as being percussionist for the wind band. Had he lived longer, who knows what he might have achieved. Over the coming weeks, I shall be consulting the student body on plans for a fitting and permanent memorial.

'Of course, it is only natural that some of you may feel . . .'

I didn't hear the rest of his speech. You'd think I'd have screamed or frothed at the mouth or something (you'd have paid good money to see that, wouldn't you, Dec?), but it was as if someone had flipped a switch and I couldn't feel anything at all. All I wanted was to sleep. And I would have done too, if a high-pitched yelping sound – a bit like the fox that stalks our street on bin nights – hadn't dragged me back to reality.

And that's when I realised that Luke Corcoran was crying.

No one said very much that first day. Even Barry the Bus Driver laid off his terrible Elvis impressions as a mark of respect.

Mum pounced the moment I walked through the

door, grabbing hold of me and refusing to let go, almost like it was me that had died. 'Your brother texted me, so they let me off work early. Oh Chris! Are you all right, my love?'

'I'm fine.'

'Poor Declan. How long had you two known each other?'

'We were at nursery together,' I said, praying she wasn't going to repeat the 'dinosaur in the sandpit' saga. 'That's . . . twelve years, isn't it?'

Mum's tears were making a damp patch on the top of my head. 'And his poor mother; do you think I should call her? Maybe it's too . . . Declan was such a lovely boy.'

You see: I told you she liked you. I know she sometimes complained you were 'eating us out of house and home', but she always kept a pepperoni pizza in the freezer 'just in case'.

'I think I'll pop upstairs, Mum.'

'Are you sure? Don't you want to come into the kitchen and talk about it?'

I shook my head.

'Well, all right then. I'll give you a call when tea's ready. I'm doing your favourite.'

And that's what it was like: everyone falling over themselves to be nice to me. I know you always said my younger brother was 'too cool for school', but even Pete interrupted his six-hour personal grooming routine to mumble that 'Declan was an OK guy'. I was actually quite glad that Dad was working late again, otherwise he would probably have got out the box set of *Top Gear* that we used to watch together when I was, like, five years old.

I auto-piloted my way through vegetable lasagne and Mum's tearful interrogation – *When's the funeral? Who was driving? What was Declan doing in that car in the first place? (Don't know, don't know . . . don't know)* – but I couldn't wait to get back to my room.

It felt strange that you weren't online. You'd have normally posted a rubbish joke by the end of *Neighbours* and even though I knew you were dead, I couldn't help double-checking to see if you'd signed in.

But you know what was even weirder? The stuff Tash Wilson and one hundred and forty-eight other friends had written on your tribute page. Darren Denyer, who peanutted you so mercilessly that you had a permanent red mark round your neck, told you to *RIP bruv*, girls who didn't even know you existed promised to *luv u 4eva bby*, and Miss Hoolyhan described you as *A wonderful young man with a fine sense of rhythm*. It was like Leonardo DiCaprio, Mother Teresa and the drummer from Rage Against The Machine had all died on the same day. Not my oldest friend, Declan.

Maybe that's why I couldn't write anything. You'd have probably come up with a killer line about painful teenage crushes, but as I stared at all the *miss u 4evas* and the *neva 4gottens* I half remembered something; something that had been buzzing around in the back of my head all day; something I was working overtime to 4get.

Two Days
After The Crash

The next day, the school was crawling with counsellors. Where they came from, I don't know. Perhaps they'd bussed them in from a war zone, because by the beginning of the second lesson, a platoon of ladies in fluffy cardigans and a couple of spiky-haired dudes were installed in the temporary classrooms, ready to listen to anyone who'd been affected by the 'tragic events of Sunday evening'.

Like it says in the prospectus, *the pastoral care at St Thomas's is second to none*, and Mr Peel, the new director of student welfare, told us to excuse ourselves from any lesson if it all got 'too heavy' and we needed to talk.

Talking was the last thing I needed, but as I wandered round the courtyard at first break, it was pretty obvious the counsellors wouldn't be short of a punter or two. Kids who would have torched their grandmothers and buried their iPads rather than show any sign of weakness were crying openly while their mates comforted them and Miss Hoolyhan and the lab technician handed out paper tissues. The Year Ten girls wore black nail varnish in your honour and everywhere I went someone seemed to be whispering your name. Don't take this the wrong way, mate, but you were a hell of a lot more popular after you'd died.

Of course, the usual suspects were telling car crash jokes outside the science block. So I sidled over, thinking I could jot down the best ones on the back of my hand. As soon as they saw me, their riotous laughter dissolved into a respectful silence. Darren Denyer even mouthed, 'Sorry, Geez,' as they drifted back into school.

That was the trouble: everyone knew we were best mates. I would normally have sold my soul (with a couple of Xbox games and an Eddie Izzard DVD thrown in) for a couple of minutes alone with Tash Wilson, but when she put her hand on my shoulder and asked me how I was doing and whether I wanted to talk about it, I told her I needed a quick browse through my science books.

It was like everyone was waiting for me to lose it; like they were surprised I hadn't put on black underpants and cried my way through double history. The fact is, I was doing fine. So long as I didn't stop to think about it, I was perfectly OK.

But it wasn't that easy. Even the teachers tried to turn

every lesson into the Declan Norris tribute show. You would have loved it. Mr Catchpole spent the first five minutes of PSHE listing ancient burial rituals. But if — according to the Polynesians — death was such a taboo subject, why was he so desperate for us to discuss it?

'Viking warriors were buried in full armour with their horse, just in case they met with battle in the afterlife,' Mr Catchpole informed us.

'I reckon Dec would want to be buried with his mobile, sir,' said Luke Corcoran. 'Do you think you get free texts on the other side?'

'That's very interesting, Luke,' said Mr Catchpole. 'What do the rest of you think? Which possessions would twenty-first century man be keenest to take with him?'

Their suggestions were as inaccurate as they were predictable: credit cards, games consoles, sixty-five varieties of fast food . . . hair straighteners. I kept my mouth shut, but I knew for a fact that if you were going to take anything it would be the only surviving copy of the first episode of that sitcom we were writing about the traffic warden with superpowers.

'Right,' said Mr Catchpole, 'can anyone tell me something about the Zoroastrians? Yes, Luke?'

Luke Corcoran never put his hand up. It was as rare as a sighting of Halley's comet. 'Oi, sir, I think I need to go and talk to a counsellor, sir.'

Mr Catchpole studied him for a moment and then

nodded. 'Yes, of course, Luke. You'd better go straight-away.'

Luke Corcoran sniffed theatrically and headed for the door.

'In some cultures, if a child died they buried a dog with them,' said Mr Catchpole, pausing for a moment in the hopes that at least one person would ask him why. 'The reason being that a dog can always find its way home. Now, the ancient Egyptians were remarkably sophisticated . . .'

Three days before I would probably have attempted a lame joke about 'yummy mummies' but as soon as he mentioned Tutankhamun, I got up from my desk and walked slowly to the door.

Rob the Slob *always* had his hand in the air. 'Sir, sir! I think something's the matter with Christopher Hughes, sir.'

I must have looked like a sleepwalker, or an Egyptian mummy on the hunt for embalming fluid. I could hear what they were saying, but it felt like one of those dreams where you lose control of your body and there's nothing you can do but go with the flow.

'It's fine,' said Mr Catchpole, stumbling to the door and holding it open for me. 'I think Christopher needs some time to sort himself out.'

I was so out of it that I barely noticed the sensational spectacle of old Cathchpole turning a blind eye to official school policy* for the one and only time in his career. (*No student may leave a lesson without permission from the supervising adult; the only exception being for peripatetic music lessons, where official procedures must be followed.)

Gliding serenely across the puddle-strewn courtyard, I was dimly aware of a trickle of miserable-looking kids on their way back from the counsellors. They can't have been doing a very good job. I mean, *I* knew you better than anybody, and I was as right as rain. But by the looks of this lot, not one of them would be going home with a happy sticker.

I wasn't sure where I was heading, but when I arrived at the Millennium Pagoda it seemed like the perfect place to bury my head in the sand.

Luke Corcoran was torturing a Year Eight with a packet of Doritos. 'Do you want them? Well, do you? Cos if you do, you're going to have to jump a lot higher than that.'

When he saw me, he looked dead ashamed and returned the tangy cheese-flavoured snacks to their rightful owner. 'Just on my way to the . . .' He pointed towards the temporary classrooms. 'See ya later, Chris.'

I squeezed into one of the picnic tables, rested my head on my folded arms and tried to concentrate on the blackness.

'Are you all right?'

I didn't move, hoping she might go away.

'I said, are you all right?'

I kept really still, trying not to breathe, like Dad did when someone knocked on the door trying to get you to change gas companies.

'Say something, Chris. You're worrying me now.'

It was that weird girl who's always reading. Some people said she belonged to a cult because she never wore designer labels and her wild, straw-coloured hair didn't change styles every fortnight. But apart from a few typical St Thomas's rumours, I didn't know that much about her. Only that she was in my set for English and her name was Ariel – which, as she told everyone at the beginning of Year Seven, is the name of a character from Shakespeare and not a washing powder.

'Look, for the last time, I'm fine, all right? Why does everyone keep asking me how I am?'

OK, I admit it – I knew something else about Ariel. I knew that you liked her. You always denied it of course, it would have been social suicide not to, but you were practically the only kid in Year Eleven who went to that talk she did on deforestation, and you didn't even crack a smile when her mum turned up to meet her from the war graves trip on a tandem. Not that I was jealous or anything. I just couldn't see why you'd want to waste your time on someone who wasn't even funny.

'You don't look fine,' she said, squeezing in opposite me. 'You look . . . weird.'

That was rich, coming from a tree hugger like Ariel. 'Thanks a lot.'

'Sorry. I know you're under a lot of pressure right now.'

'Pressure, what pressure?'

'You and Dec were really close. He was always talking about you.'

I wasn't that keen on the idea of you and her having cosy chats about me. 'What's that got to do with any thing?'

'Look, I don't mean to be rude, Chris . . .' When people say that it's usually exactly what they mean. '. . . but can't you see you're behaving a bit . . . strangely?'

I'd rather have spent ten minutes with one of the fluffy-cardiganed counsellors. Half of me felt drawn to her; the sensible half already realised how dumb that was. 'I don't know what you're talking about.'

'It's just that . . .' She turned away from me, fixing her attention on the all-weather hockey pitches. 'You don't seem very . . . upset. I mean, I've hardly stopped crying for the last two days, but you . . .'

We sat in silence for the longest two minutes of my life. If she didn't go soon, there was a distinct possibility I might start thinking again.

'I don't get it . . .' I started. 'What was he . . . I mean, why did he . . . How did it . . .?'

Ariel tugged at the cuffs of her fingerless gloves. 'They say he got into a car with a bunch of Sixth Form college kids.'

'And had the driver been drinking or something?' I said, anxious for someone to blame.

'Don't know.' Ariel shrugged. 'Could have been; it was getting pretty messy in there.'

'How do *you* know?'

'Well, because . . .' she licked her glossless lips, 'because I was at the party.' It was the first time I'd seen a girl cry without creating black rivers of mascara. 'I told him he could walk home with me and Mum, but it was pouring with rain and he said he could get a lift.'

Ariel was about as close to being a party animal as I was to being good at PE. She'd already told anyone who'd listen that she wouldn't be seen dead at the prom because she couldn't understand why any sixteen year olds would want to dress up like a bunch of 'middle-aged bank managers and their wives'.

'I thought you hated parties.'

'Sometimes they're OK,' she said, turning back towards the all-weather hockey pitches and sniffing. 'Depends who you're with.'

'And, anyway, didn't the crash happen out near Blackthorn Farm? That's nowhere near Declan's house. What was the driver playing at?'

'Probably showing off,' said Ariel, her voice cracking,

like it did in English when she felt particularly strongly about something – which she often did. 'That's what boys do, isn't it?'

I remembered her giving Tash Wilson a hard time for assuming the pilot in *Lord of the Flies* was a man. Considering the plane had crashed, I didn't think it was sexist at all. 'If you say so.'

'Dec wasn't like that though, was he?'

I wondered where she'd been for the last four years.

'Once you got to know him, he was actually quite a deep thinker.'

Perhaps some other Declan Norris had died recently.

Ariel's balloon-debating voice turned to a hoarse whisper. 'He didn't deserve to . . . you know. Did he, Chris?'

I had to get away before I started thinking any deeper myself. 'Gotta go,' I said, jumping – almost athletically – to my feet. 'There's a science assessment I need to revise for.'

'Chris, wait,' she called. 'Don't you want to . . .? Look, there's something I need to tell you.'

But I was already on my way to the field. And I only stopped running when I came to that muddy football pitch where you, me and the other 'low achievers' spent many a soggy afternoon hiding from the ball and winding up that PE teacher by calling table tennis 'ping pong'.

I know of at least one person who could come up

with some wacky explanation for what I did next. Actually, I think I just wanted to hear your voice – *just like I can hear you laughing now, smart arse.*

Your answerphone message was usually dead annoying, especially as, no matter how many times I heard it, it always caught me out. This time I didn't mind because, just for a second or two, I could almost believe you were still alive.

'Hi . . . hi, you'll have to speak up I . . . I can't hear you. No . . . no . . . I still can't . . . [You do two blasts of your depressingly brilliant Woody Woodpecker laugh.] *Gotcha!* Hi, this is Declan speaking. If you've got something funny to say, leave me a message. Otherwise, hang up when you hear the beep.'

And that's when I felt my first twinge of pain.

Five Days
After The Crash

The whole thing was Mr Catchpole's idea. The school had been disrupted for long enough and this was a way of 'moving forward', 'achieving closure,' etc, etc. It was also 'what Declan would have wanted'. That was a phrase we heard a lot back then. I was too dazed to object, otherwise I would have told him that a 'celebration' of your life in the sports hall was the last thing you'd have wanted, and there would have been absolutely no way I'd have agreed to take part in the ridiculous finale.

'Today is not about grieving,' said the Demon Headmaster, his radio mike squealing in agony, 'but about giving thanks for a life lived to the full.'

You hadn't done half the stuff you wanted. You'd never solved the Countdown conundrum, Angelina Jolie was still in a relationship, your tireless quest for the perfect pepperoni pizza had barely started, and that dream we had of taking our double-act to the Edinburgh Festival was well and truly knackered.

'Declan Norris was an inspiration for many of you here this morning. We want to celebrate his achievements, as well as acknowledge that he will be sorely missed.'

The junior choir sung 'The Circle of Life' (which you claimed was compulsory at all school events), the wind band played 'Yesterday', a kid called Matthew Layton did a terrible song called 'Death Blows/Life Sucks', and Rob the Slob read a poem about dead people just being in the next room.

Those of us who'd been chosen waited under the basketball net, mentally rehearsing our speeches and trying to keep still while Mr Peel and his helpers attached microphones to our jacket pockets. I could see why Tash Wilson might have been selected: she had the lead part in the school play where you were the voice of the killer plant. But I couldn't for the life of me see what Ariel was doing there. I'd been making a pretty good job of avoiding her. That's why I pretended to be wiping my eyes when she looked across and smiled at me.

The Demon Headmaster sounded relieved that it was nearly over. 'Declan touched the lives of so many of us. We've heard from Miss Hoolyhan about his exuberant maracas playing, but it's only right that the last word should go to those of you who knew him best – his fellow students.'

'OK, guys,' whispered Mr Peel. 'This is it.'

We trooped onto the temporary stage at the front of the sports hall and formed a straggly line. I don't remember feeling nervous. All I remember is thinking that if *you'd* been there it would have been the biggest audience we'd ever played to.

First up was a rabbit-in-the-footlights Year Seven. He unfolded a piece of paper and stumbled his way through a couple of painful sentences: 'Declan was . . . my . . . reading . . . mentor. I never . . . liked . . . reading much, but Declan . . . found me a book . . . about a boy with an . . . exploding bottom . . . which was . . . cool.'

Tash Wilson's speech contained several inaccuracies, which I'm sure I don't have to spell out for you: 'The thing that was so great about him was that he always had this amazing smile on his face. Everyone liked Dec. He'd do anything for you. He was the funniest guy I've ever met.' (We all knew that Tash could cry for England.) 'Rest in peace, Declan. We'll never forget you.'

I was trying to remember your one-liner about the man in the electric chair when Ariel stepped forward. She was the last one before me, and I was starting to have serious doubts about opening with a gag.

Ariel opened with a bombshell of her own. 'Declan

and I had only being going out for three weeks, but I'm proud to say he was my boyfriend.'

Remember that Saturday afternoon we spent working on our double takes? You should have seen my jaw hit the stage; it was perfect.

'Declan was a man for all seasons,' said Ariel. 'Yes, he was funny, but he was so, *so* much more than that. Declan cared. He cared about the environment, and he cared about his friends. And he loved nature. Whenever I see a charm of finches bursting into the September sky – that's when I'll remember him.' I could see how hard she was working not to cry. 'Declan didn't deserve to die. I know it was an accident. It's just . . . well, it would be a whole lot easier if I could find someone to blame. I'm sorry, I . . . sorry . . .'

Miss Hoolyhan handed her a tissue as she fled from the stage.

So why didn't you tell me, Declan? We were supposed to be best mates. If I'd known you were into bird watching, the jokes would have written themselves.

'OK, Chris,' whispered Mr Peel. 'It's your turn next, fella.'

I shuffled forward, staring out into the cavernous sports hall. Approximately two thousand, four hundred eyes stared back at me. At first I thought there were technical problems – something wrong with the sound system – because when I opened my mouth, I couldn't hear a thing.

But it was more serious than that. No matter how hard I tried, I just couldn't get my words out.

I told myself it was some bizarre form of stage fright, and it wasn't until after Miss Hoolyhan had led me from the stage and plied me with milky tea in the staffroom that I knew it for certain: I was completely dumb.

Three Weeks After The Crash

Your funeral wasn't at all how we'd planned it. I wasn't dressed as Adolf Hitler for a start, Angelina didn't turn up in her Lara Croft outfit, and when your coffin slid down the conveyor belt to the great comedy club in the sky, all we got was dreary organ music and not the theme tune from *Austin Powers*.

It was another full house though. I didn't recognise most of them, but your mum and dad sat scrunched up together at the front, like they were trying to keep warm in the snow, and that drama teacher with pink hair made a dramatic entrance just before the coffin.

Rob the Slob had a dual role that morning, as the Demon Headmaster's representative on earth and as my rather reluctant minder. 'Is my tie straight, Christopher?' he whispered as six moustachioed men death-marched down the aisle with a brown box on their shoulders. 'I said, is my tie straight?'

Like that was ever going to work.

Ariel was three rows in front of us with Miss Hoolyhan. She tried to catch my attention, but I pretended to be revising the order of service.

'*I became dumb, and opened not my mouth: for it was thy doing. Take thy plague away from me. I am even . . .*'

There were no jokes in it, I can promise you that. On the plus side, the vicar guy said so many nice things about you that I felt like checking the coffin to make sure they'd got the right person, your sister drove all the way from Norwich specially to sing 'Amazing Grace' and Rob the Slob did a poem about dead people just being in the next room. Come to think of it, I'd rather be properly dead than stuck in the spare bedroom for all eternity.

Everything seemed to be going fine until after the funeral service, when Rob the Slob decided he needed to 'inspect the facilities' before escorting me back to school. And I was feigning an interest in the row of flowers outside the crematorium, hoping no one would try and talk to me, when I felt an icy hand on my shoulder.

'Hello, Chris, I'm so glad you could make it.'

It was the same black dress she'd worn for your Halloween party – although without the fangs and fake blood. You've got to believe me, Declan, I really wanted to say something to her. The night before the funeral I'd stood in front of the bathroom mirror, twisting my mouth into the shapes that would make the right words. Even in private, I couldn't manage a solitary syllable. As soon as I saw the anguish in your mum's sleep-starved eyes, I knew it was impossible.

'It's all right,' she said, reaching out and squeezing my arm. 'I know you can't . . . I just wanted to tell you that . . .'

Which reminds me, Declan, I probably ought to mention that your mum and dad moved to Norwich. I try not to walk past your old house any more. There's a trampoline in the garden and a 4x4 in the drive.

'. . . Dec wouldn't have wanted you to mope around like this. Dec would have wanted you to get on with your life. Will you do that for me?'

That was the trouble: everyone assumed that the only reason I couldn't talk was because my best friend had died. Unfortunately, it was rather more complicated than that.

Everyone was convinced it was only temporary. Our GP, Dr Worrall, assured Mum that with a bit of counselling, and so long as no one pressured me, it was only a matter of time before I found my voice again. But until that happened, Mum had the bright idea of sending me back to school with a set of index cards inscribed with such useful phrases as *No, thank you*, *Spicy sausage pasta, please* and *Luke Corcoran has purloined my protractor and put peanuts in my pencil case.* (OK, I made the last one up.) 'Well, you won't do it,' she said, already struggling to conceal her frustration. 'At least this way you won't go hungry.'

School really wasn't that bad. A certain staffroom amateur psychologist (that's right Declan, Mr Catchpole, who else could it be?) made the mistake of trying to get me to 'jot down a few notes' about my feelings, but as soon as the teachers realised that the only writing I was remotely capable of was my GSCE coursework, they stopped hassling me and left me to it.

If only the other kids had been the same. In the days after you'd died, they talked about you the whole time. Hardly a lesson went by when someone didn't come out with a 'Declan would have done so and so' or 'Remember that time Declan . . .?' But gradually your name cropped up less and less until one afternoon I realised that no one had mentioned it at all. You'd been dead three weeks, don't forget. My brother Pete had been through two serious relationships since then, so it was hardly surprising that even the ones who'd sobbed the most spectacularly were ready to 'move on'. And by that I mean they were ready to move on to me.

To begin with, they'd followed Mr Peel's instruction to 'give the poor guy some space', but then, one history lesson, someone made a joke about how brilliant I'd have been in a silent movie, and it wasn't long before they were taking bets on who could be the first one to get me to talk. Everywhere I went there was a camera phone in my face, its owner hell bent on recording the historic moment and putting it on Facebook.

Part of me wanted to oblige, if only with a polite, 'I'm fine, thank you for your concern,' or a not-so-polite, 'Get out of my face, you loser,' but even when I attempted a few words in the privacy of my own bedroom, they stuck in my throat like a shark in a boa constrictor.

And when I went to the canteen after the funeral, it seemed like half of Year Eleven had surrounded me and my spicy sausage pasta by the time I sat down to eat.

'Oi, Slobber,' said Luke Corcoran. 'He didn't say nothing, did he?'

Rob the Slob shook his head and pretended to be in the next room.

That was everyone's cue to start firing questions. It was like a rubbish game show where the sole aim of the contestants was to trick me into speaking.

'Hey, Chris, what's the time?'

'Who's the Prime Minister?'

'Where's the best place to buy metal detectors?'

'What's the next lesson?'

'Knock, knock.'

'Is that spicy sausage or cheese and tomato?'

Tash Wilson played her 'joker', pulling her chair so

close our legs were almost touching. 'Hey, Chris, do you want to go out sometime? All you've got to do is say the word.'

'What makes you think he wants to go out with you, anyway?' said that girl who threw up on the war graves trip.

'He's a bloke, isn't he?' said Tash.

'Let's hear it from the man himself,' said Luke Corcoran, tomato ketchup trickling down his bottom lip. 'Go on, Chris . . . speech!'

And the others joined in, banging their plastic forks on the tables and stamping their feet. '*Speech, speech, speech, speech, speech . . .*'

Remember all those putdowns we worked on to deal with hecklers? It was the first time I really needed one, and yet all I could do was stare into the vending machine and glow bright pink.

'*Speech, speech, speech . . .*'

I'd managed to make it to the end of the funeral without feeling anything, but I wasn't even halfway through my pot of pasta and already I was in danger of losing it.

'*Speech, speech, speech . . .*'

I was about to do a runner when a loud, clear voice cut across their frenzied chanting. 'Shut up! Shut up the lot of you. Do you think it's funny or something? Well, do you?'

It wasn't as good as 'Let's hear it for the only surviving brain transplant donor' or 'If I throw a stick will you leave?', but it seemed to do the trick. Only Luke Corcoran let out a half-hearted, 'It *is* pretty funny as it goes, yeah.'

Ariel gave him the same look she'd given me when I suggested that *Romeo and Juliet* would work better as a sitcom. 'Have you forgotten already?' she said, swooping on him like a peregrine falcon. 'His best friend died *three weeks ago*. Why can't you just leave him alone?'

Luke Corcoran smirked silently and licked tomato sauce from his lips.

'He can't help it, you know,' said Ariel, dropping her voice as if I was in the next room and not slap bang in front of her. 'I'm not sure what it's all about – this silence business – but I *do* know that it's serious. The last thing Chris needs is you lot making it any harder.'

Most of them looked suitably ashamed, but Tash Wilson and Ariel had 'history'. 'Well, good old Miss Amnesty International,' said Tash. 'Aren't we lucky to have a saint in our midst? Like your hair by the way. Did Mummy cut it for you?'

'Who did your nails,' said Luke Corcoran. 'The Handy Man Shop?'

'Come on, Chris,' said Ariel. 'Let's get you out of here.'

I wasn't thrilled at the prospect of taking orders from my deceased best friend's ex, but nor did I fancy another round of 'Get the lunatic to talk'. So I swallowed a final forkful of spicy sausage and followed Ariel out to the courtyard.

'What a load of idiots,' she said, attempting to tame her unruly hair. 'You shouldn't take any notice of them.'

She was the only girl at St Thomas's who wore hand-knitted jumpers. I tried to figure out exactly what you'd seen in her.

'If you ever feel like getting away from it all, Chris, you could always hang out at mine for a bit. Declan *said* he wanted us to be friends.'

That I doubted very much.

'I wouldn't try to make you talk or anything,' she said, stamping on a stray crisp packet and despatching it to the rubbish bin. 'We could take a walk round the wetlands if you like. You know where I live, don't you?'

Would that have been the feminist candle-making collective or the Buddhist retreat?

'It's about twenty minutes from the town centre. You follow the path by the river and turn right when you see the sign for the nature reserve. We're right behind the beetle loggery. Why don't you walk over at half-term?'

My fake smile was designed to suggest I might even be thinking about it. Actually, I was still seething about something she'd said in the canteen. Not being able to talk was certainly inconvenient, but as long as no one expected me to write an essay about my feelings or make a speech in French about *La Vie Scolaire*, I could still get my coursework in on time. And I wasn't best pleased that Ariel was going round telling everyone I had a 'serious' problem. At least, that's what I tried to convince myself then.

Of course, it was only a matter of time before I realised she was right.

Three and a Half Weeks
After The Crash

Psychiatrist: I'm sorry to have to tell you this,
but I'm afraid you're absolutely mad.
Patient: I want a second opinion.
Psychiatrist: You're ugly too.

It was my first session at the CAMHS (Child and Adolescent Mental Health Service) office. Mum was dressed for a royal wedding, not a visit to the child psychiatrist.

'Hi, my name's Dr Tennant,' said the lady in the flowery top, 'but I'd prefer it if you called me Kim.'

Her office didn't inspire much confidence. There was a wooden doll's house in the corner, a bucket of chewed-up Lego and a whiteboard with a graph demonstrating the different phases of anxiety using cartoons of baseball-capped teenagers spouting speech bubbles with swear words in them.

'Now, I've had a referral from your GP, but maybe you should start by telling me something about yourself.'

Mum twitched nervously. 'That's the point, Kim. He can't talk – or *won't* talk, we're not sure which. Surely Dr Worrall mentioned it in his letter?'

'Yes, yes of course,' said Dr Tennant. (Even in my head, I couldn't bring myself to call her Kim.) 'But we sometimes find our clients respond differently in a . . . clinical environment.'

It was clinical all right. Dad's desk was covered with pictures of me, Mum and Pete, but here there wasn't a family photograph in sight. What was the use of a child psychiatrist who didn't have children herself?

'Perhaps you'd like to tell me something about school?'

I was getting used to long silences. It was Dr Tennant who seemed most relieved when the door flew open.

'Sorry, sorry . . . I'm really sorry. I tried to get away early, but there's trouble oop at mill.'

Dad was so terrified of being made redundant that he spent half his life at the office.

'That's quite all right,' said Dr Tennant. 'Perhaps we'd better move on to Christopher's medical history. Was it an easy pregnancy?'

It's surprising how much of my medical history was

bound up with yours: the chickenpox outbreak at nursery, that time you dared me to stick a peanut in my ear, the incident with the miniature hot air balloon. But I still couldn't see what any of it had to do with my 'problem'.

Dr Tennant obviously thought otherwise. 'And is there any history of, er . . . mental illness in the family?'

'Certainly not,' said Dad, his eyes flaring like a lunatic's.

And it was all going great until she gave us the *Strengths and Difficulties Questionnaire* to fill in. It was kind of like one of those quizzes in Mum's magazines (*Are You a Morning Person?*, *How Stressed Is Your Pet?*) where you have to decide if a statement is *Not True*, *Somewhat True* or *Certainly True*, except that in this case all the statements were about me.

'Considerate of other people's feelings?' said Mum, sucking the top of her ballpoint. 'I think that's a *Certainly True*.'

Dad checked his watch. 'He's never terribly considerate about texting us when he's running late. I'm talking about before the . . . well, you know.'

'Come on, Chris,' said Mum, trying to jolly me along. 'Don't just sit there like a dead parrot. You're supposed to be helping . . . What do *you* think?'

I was trying hard not to.

'All right,' said Mum, disappointedly. 'We'll say *Somewhat True*, shall we? Now, *Restless, overactive, cannot stay still long?*'

Somehow I made it through a couple more statements,

until Mum looked down at the next one, and the colour drained from her face, like a vampire in need of a blood transfusion. 'Oh dear.'

'Well, come on, Pauline,' said Dad, who was starting to get into it. 'Keep them coming.'

'*Has at least one good friend,*' whispered Mum.

Dad reached for her hand. 'This is what it's all about you see, doctor. Chris had a very close friend . . . Declan. But he . . . well, he . . . he had an accident, you see.'

Dr Tennant smiled professionally. 'Yes, I know. It's in his notes. What can you tell me about Declan?'

Sorry, Dec; I'm sure you'd love to hear what they said about you, but the next bit's kind of blurry, so I only got the gist: '*Known each other since nursery school – hardly ever apart – fancied himself as bit of a joker – almost* too *close if you ask me.*'

Because that's when it hit me: a sadness so over-whelming it felt like all the lights in the universe were going out. It was the first time I'd really accepted it: that we'd never go to sixth form college together, never write another joke, that Declan Norris really *had* left the building – and you were never coming back.

Somewhere out in space, I heard Mum's voice. 'Chris, Chrissie, love, are you all right?'

It started in my little finger, spread quickly to my arms and up through my torso, until my whole body was shaking so violently it must have looked like a macabre new form of street dance. Even the Lego figures on Dr Tennant's desk were jigging along with me. And yes, there were tears too as I surrendered myself to that excruciating feeling.

But it wasn't grief; grief I could have learnt to cope with. It was so much worse than that. As if a black cloud of my own making was parked permanently above my head. All I knew was that I'd done something terrible; something so terrible, I simply wasn't ready to face it yet. And even in my head, I was about a million miles away from being able to put it into words.

So I threw back my head and howled.

After she'd managed to calm me down and I was dabbing my face with her lipstick-stained tissue, Mum rounded angrily on Dr Tennant. 'And you honestly think this is helping?'

'I know it's difficult,' she said, glancing at the half-completed questionnaire, 'but I really think Chris has made a breakthrough here. I could be wrong, but I have a feeling he may be ready to communicate.'

'Really?' said Mum, hopefully.

'I just want a quick word with your parents, Chris,' said Dr Tennant, 'so, we're going to pop outside for a moment and give you some space.' She handed me a sheet of paper and a stubby pencil scarred with the tooth marks of her previous victims. 'Perhaps you'd like to write it all down – your feelings about Declan; why you can't seem to share them with anybody.'

'We have tried this you know,' said Mum. 'He just refuses point blank to communicate. It's so frustrating, isn't it, Trevor?'

Dr Tennant scrawled illegibly in her bulging page-a-day diary. 'As I say, Christopher might respond better in a different setting. Let's leave him to it, shall we?'

She tried the 'paper torture' every week. Later on I learned to cope with it. But that first time, I stared at the shiny piece of A4 like it was that Year Ten statistics paper with the question on cumulative frequency. If I couldn't talk about it, what made her think I'd want to see it written down? In the end, I did what I would always do: ripped it into tiny pieces and tossed them in the air like confetti.

All I knew was that I never wanted to feel like that again. And since psychiatry was far more excruciating than I'd ever imagined, I figured it was time to give something else a chance. What I needed was a distraction; anything that could take my mind off that terrible feeling.

Five Weeks
After The Crash

Half the class was *definitely* distracted. An audible tremor of female admiration circled the humanities suite as the tall, dark stranger breezed into English and posed in front of the whiteboard, like a movie star on the red carpet generously allowing a photo opportunity.

'Hi, gang,' said Mr Peel, who stood at his side, like an ageing co-star, attempting to bask in his reflected glory. 'How are you travelling?'

'On the bus,' came a voice from the back.

Standards of student witticism had plummeted dramatically since you died.

Mr Peel smiled lamely and picked a dog hair off his brown leather jacket. 'OK, listen up, because there's a guy here I really want you to meet. This is Will. He's going to be with us for the rest of Year Eleven. Now, it's not easy being the new kid on the block, yeah? So I hope you're all going to give him a big St Thomas's welcome.'

The traditional sound of one hand clapping didn't seem to bother the handsome newcomer. He stepped forward, palm raised, like a politician at a press conference.

'First up, I'd like to thank you all for welcoming me to the school.'

He spoke like a politician too. But although his accent was unusual by St Thomas's standards, it wasn't his most striking feature. His impressive mane of thick black hair – pointed like a lapwing at the back and tumbling over his forehead like a waterfall at the front – may have looked random, but I knew from observing my brother that it was the product of many hours intensive grooming.

'Like Mr Peel said, my name's Will – Will Hunt. Believe it or not, this is my first time in state education. But I hope you won't hold it against me, because underneath I'm actually a pretty nice guy – or so my mum tells me.' He bared a set of pearly white teeth. 'Now, does anyone have any questions?'

'Why did you leave your last school?' asked Rob the Slob.

'No comment,' said Will Hunt, sounding even more like a politician.

'Would you like me to show you round at lunchtime?' said Tash Wilson.

The newcomer flashed his teeth again. 'That's really nice of you, but I've already had the grand tour.'

'I could take you to the canteen if you like,' said the girl who puked on the war graves trip.

'If anyone takes him it should be me,' said Rob the Slob. 'I'm the head student.'

'Let's have a bit of quiet, shall we?' said Mrs Woolf, almost living up to her nickname for once. 'Look, it's nice to meet you, Will, but we really need to crack on.'

'OK, guys, I'll leave you to it,' said Mr Peel. 'And look after Will, yeah? I've been telling him what a cool bunch you are.'

The Big Bad Woolf looked delighted to be back in charge. 'Sit down would you, Will? There's a space next to Christopher.'

There was an empty seat to my left in practically every lesson. From what I'd seen, Will Hunt was the last person I'd have chosen to fill it.

'All right, matey?' he said, plonking himself down next to me and stretching his legs.

I nodded, hoping against hope he wouldn't try to make conversation.

'We've been studying Arthur Miller's classic play, *The Crucible*,' said Mrs Woolf. 'Who can tell Will some of the principle themes?'

It didn't matter *what* we were studying, someone always suggested it. 'Is it about loss of innocence, Miss?'

Mrs Woolf winced and closed her eyes as if in silent prayer. 'Surely someone has been paying attention for the last six weeks?'

It was Ariel who sprang to the rescue. I'd done my best to steer clear of her, but she was obstinately refusing to get off my case. If ever we passed in the corridor, she launched into a Declan story or reminded me of her invitation to hang out at half-term.

'*The Crucible* is based on the Salem witch trials of 1692,' she said, 'with the obvious parallel of the so-called communist witch hunts in 1950s America.'

I can't pretend I wasn't tempted by Ariel's offer. In a way it would have been nice to hear someone talking about you again, Dec. But that visit to the psychiatrist was a real wake-up call. If I started fraternising with your ex-girlfriend, who knows what feelings it might unleash?

'It's about what happens when mass hysteria takes over,' she continued. 'How weak, powerless individuals find ways of acting on old grudges when they suddenly feel empowered by the mob.'

'And it's about the way we like to label people,' added the girl who puked on the war graves trip. 'If you can find yourself a scapegoat, *that's* when the hysteria starts.'

'Sounds like a right barrel of laughs,' said Will Hunt.

'It's not supposed to be funny,' said Ariel. 'Didn't you hear? It's a classic play.'

The newcomer looked surprised at the fury he'd unleashed. 'Sorry; didn't mean to upset anyone.'

'Don't worry, Will,' said Tash Wilson. 'Poor Ariel had a sense of humour bypass in Year Seven.'

'That's enough,' said Mrs Woolf. 'Now I want to look at the first scene of Act Two. Tash could you read Elizabeth please? And Will, perhaps you'd like to read John Proctor?'

'Not a good idea, I'm afraid.'

Mrs Woolf wasn't sure if she'd heard him right. 'I'm sorry?'

'I wish I could,' said Will, 'but I have this terrible problem with dyslexia.' He flashed me a sly wink. 'On my mother's side.'

'Really?' said Mrs Woolf. 'Well, it's the first I've heard of it. I'd better have a word with our inclusion coordinator.'

'Good idea,' said Will, 'but in the meantime, why not let Christopher have a go? He's hardly said a word all morning.'

It was Rob the Slob who broke the edgy silence. 'That would be difficult, I'm afraid. You see, Christopher doesn't talk.'

'This is a joke, right?' said Will. 'I know I'm the newbie, but I wasn't born yesterday.'

'It's true,' said Rob the Slob. 'He's been unable – or unwilling – to communicate for a few weeks.'

'Wow,' said Will, flicking his fringe from his face

with a swift jerk of the head. 'You mean the poor guy's completely dumb?'

It was the first time that anyone had used the d-word. It was only later that I realised how appropriate it was.

'It's not funny you know,' snapped Ariel, 'and don't you dare call him that. It's really offensive.'

'Yeah, course,' said Will. 'I'll bear it in mind.'

Mrs Woolf reached for her liquorice allsorts earrings. 'All right, Robert, you can read Proctor and Tash, you're Elizabeth. Now just get on with it.'

Just as Rob the Slob's monotonous reading voice was sending me into a dreamy coma, a sharp dig in the ribs brought me back to reality. 'Nice one, mate,' whispered Will Hunt. 'I like your style.'

I didn't know what he was talking about, but one thing was very clear. Will Hunt was definitely another name for my 'to avoid' list. Luckily, there wasn't a chance in hell that a player like him would ever be seen dead with a silent comedian like me.

At first break, they clustered round him in the canteen, allowing me to enjoy my spicy sausage pasta in peace.

Will Hunt seemed to be enjoying the attention. 'Can anyone tell me what on *earth* that last lesson was all about?'

'PHSE,' said Tash Wilson. 'It's the same every week.'

'It was so unbelievably boring, I felt like trying some of those "terrible" things, just to keep awake.' He mimed an exaggerated yawn. 'And what's with that ridiculous Catchpole person?'

'He's quite a good teacher, actually,' said Rob the Slob loyally.

'I'm sure he is,' said Will, 'but it's not exactly cutting edge, is it? At my last school, we had a fully-fledged happiness and well-being policy.'

Ariel was sitting at the next table with her nose in a paperback. 'So why didn't you stay there, then?'

Will smiled benevolently. 'It's Ariel, isn't it? Look, I'm really sorry if we got off on the wrong foot. Now, is there something you wanted to ask me?'

'I think she wants to know why you left your last school,' said Rob the Slob.

Will downed his OJ and licked his lips. 'Good question. I didn't want to say anything in front of the screws,' he glanced across at the lucky teacher on dinner duty, 'but to tell you the truth, I was, what I think you lot would call, permanently excluded.'

'Respect,' said Luke Corcoran. 'What did they do you for?'

'It's not something I'm particularly proud of – and I'm certainly not suggesting you should try it here – but me and some of the guys hacked into the school intranet and changed all the exam results. Actually, it was a really good laugh. Unfortunately Miss Mackenzie-Brooks didn't see it that way.'

'Miss who?' said Luke Corcoran.

'She's the head of my old school. You've probably seen her on telly. She made that documentary on Pitt the Elder. And she's always got something in the paper about how to improve state education.'

'Yeah, that's right,' sneered Ariel. 'I forgot Luke was a *Telegraph* reader.'

'Anyway,' said Will, not quite managing to disguise his irritation, 'the point is, *I* took the rap, and Ed and Jake got off with a caution. The whole school turned up at the station to see me off.'

'You're so nice,' said the girl who puked on the war graves trip.

Rob the Slob was thoughtfully mopping up crumbs with his spare handkerchief. 'I don't understand. Wouldn't that be a bit —?'

'Hey, Will,' said Tash Wilson, ramming a ten ton pick-up truck into the Slob's train of thought. 'Why don't you come down Purgatory with us on Friday night? It's pretty rubbish, and the music's crap, but I'm sure we could show you a good time.'

'I'd love to,' said Will. 'Unfortunately, I'm pretty much permanently grounded right now.'

Rob the Slob's train of thought was slowly pulling into the station. 'I just can't see why it would be allowed – the whole school. It sounds a bit —'

'Anyway,' said Will, 'tell me about Christopher.' He

flicked his fringe in my direction. 'What's the matter with him? Is it physical, or is he mental or something?'

'No one really knows,' said Tash Wilson. 'He sort of clammed up after his best friend died.'

Will whistled appreciatively. 'No wonder he looks so miserable. What happened? Another shanking, I suppose?'

'Car accident,' said Tash Wilson. 'Poor Declan was the one who really suffered, but this one has been acting strangely ever since.'

'Would you mind not talking about him like he isn't there?' said Ariel.

Rob the Slob stepped in to keep the peace. 'We've tried everything to get him to open up, but he just won't say a word.'

'Maybe I could do something,' said Will, suddenly standing to attention and clicking his heels. 'Ve have vays of making you tork!'

Ariel was about the only person in the canteen not laughing. 'Oh yes, really mature.'

'No one seems to know if he'll ever speak again,' said Rob the Slob.

Will Hunt smiled quietly to himself, just like you would after you'd thought of a new gag. 'So it's a bit of a mystery, eh?' And then he sung the next bit, like it was the end of a scene in a rubbish horror movie. 'Dumb de dumb dumb, DUMB!'

Even I had to admit that standards of student witticism had risen significantly since Will Hunt arrived.

'The guy's a legend,' said Luke Corcoran. 'Great hair n'all.'

Now please don't take this the wrong way, Declan, but I want to run it past you because I have a feeling it might explain a lot. You see, in a strange sense, I think Will reminded me of you – the funny voices, the way he loved to make people laugh. I noticed something else about him too. After the bell went and they'd abandoned him to his ham and tomato panini, he seemed to shrink, right in front of my very eyes. Just like you, Declan, he really came alive in front of an audience.

And then there were three: Ariel, ploughing doggedly on to the end of her chapter, Will Hunt, suddenly looking every inch the lonely new boy, and your old mate Chris Hughes, *still* not talking.

Seven Weeks
After The Crash

Half-term turned out to be more like living under house arrest. They'd really stepped up security since my first visit to the CAMHS office. Mum typed out a special set of holiday cards with such useful phrases as *Gone to the library* and *Popped out to OneStop*. It was her − not so subtle − way of trying to control my movements. Even so, I had zilch all chance of participating in any of those thrilling activities without close adult supervision because Mum and Dad were taking it in turns to stay home with me. They let Pete slink off to Brighton every morning with his mate Gary Lulham, so how come they were so desperate to endure a whole week of 'quality time' with *me*?

I spent the first morning in my bedroom watching our favourite movies. None of them seemed particularly funny. I know it was about the twenty-fourth time I'd watched them, but we'd laughed non-stop at our last comedy marathon. And it was the same when I dusted off our sitcom. Maybe *The Capped Crusader* wasn't such a brilliant title after all, and some of the jokes were practically prehistoric.

So I was actually quite glad when Dad called me down for lunch. It was only when he started outlining his plans for the afternoon's entertainment that my heart sank like the middle of one of Mum's Christmas cakes.

'We could get Monopoly out if you like. And we've still got a whole season of *The Wire* to watch.'

I couldn't believe his dreaded Sales Director had actually agreed to let him work from home for the week.

'Tell you what, why don't I take you down the park for a kick around?'

And I thought *I* was the one who was supposed to be crazy.

'Yes, all right,' said Dad, who still looked half-asleep after his third mug of coffee, 'silly suggestion. Maybe we could get a pumpkin and hollow it out for Halloween – just like the old days.'

I'm sure you can guess my reaction to *that* idea.

'Look, this is hard for me too, you know,' said Dad. 'I really want to help you, son, but you've got to work with me here. You don't know what all this is doing to your mother. For God's sake, Christopher, say something . . . PLEASE.' Dad was the same with foreigners: he seemed to think that shouting would make them understand him better. 'Sorry, sorry, I didn't mean to . . .'

Dad's ringtone had irritated and embarrassed me ever since I hit thirteen, but never before had I been so glad to hear the theme tune from *Match of the Day*.

'Hi, Dominic,' said Dad, turning instantaneously from suicidal parent to employee of the month. 'What can I do for you? No, of course you're not . . . Absolutely . . . No no no, he's fine . . . not a problem.' His telephone smile looked more like a botched facelift. 'Sorry, son,' he whispered. 'I'll have to take this one upstairs.'

I would have done almost anything to avoid another second of quality time with Dad. So ten minutes later, I Blu-tacked a card reading *Going for a short walk* to the back of the letterbox, and slipped out the front door.

He might have been a pretty good account manager, but Dad would have made a rubbish spook. Every time I looked round, I saw his orange ski jacket duck down behind a postbox or freeze in front of a window display.

He was always saying how unfit teenagers were, how he'd spent the first fifteen years of his life kicking a ball around, so, when we got to the shopping centre, it was time to test his legendary powers of endurance. You've seen me sprinting, Declan; I'm not exactly Usain Bolt. But by the time I'd run up the escalator, side-stepped the Sky TV man and circled the sinister singing Santa and his elves (Mum called it 'scandalous' that he was already crooning 'White Christmas' in October), Dad was taking a crafty breather on the bench outside Laura Ashley. Unfortunately, ditching Dad was the easy part.

Deep down, I think I always knew where I was headed. It was only when I came to the river that I stopped kidding myself it was a random mystery tour. The town nature reserve (and wetlands wildlife trail) was free for anyone under sixteen, presumably because no one that age would be crazy enough to want to go there. Even so, I took a map from the information centre, hurried through the evil-smelling organic café and followed the yellow signs for the beetle loggery.

I don't know what I was expecting; at least a giant beetle or two, not just a pathetic collection of mouldy tree stumps. And I didn't spend the next five minutes reading about the life cycle of the stag beetle because half a decade munching through dead wood sounded like great material for an autobiography. I did it because I was scared; scared that I was getting into something I might later regret.

There was no sign of life anyway, just a muddy path and a tangled wilderness of naked trees and prickly bushes. It was only when I looked down and saw the small hand-painted sign bearing the name *HONESTY* that I knew I'd come to the right place.

Like you said, procrastination is what I'm best at, and it was a good five minutes before I began forcing my way through the undergrowth, struggling to keep upright in the soupy quagmire and almost blinding myself in the process. It felt like the road to nowhere until the path widened, the squelch beneath my trainers turned into a gentle crunch and I stepped out into the light.

I bet even you were surprised the first time you saw it, Declan. Double the size of a football pitch, the plot was surrounded on three sides by trees, with a swampy area at the bottom leading to the lake. A complex walk-way of wooden planks divided the different vegetable patches. Most of them lay dormant, but I noticed several rows of that nasty green stuff Mum claims 'puts hairs on your chest'.

A thin plume of smoke rose from the white caravan at the far end and drifted up into a clear blue sky. Chickens were wandering freely in front of the rickety woodshed, alongside what looked like a sheep and a couple of geese. It reminded me of one of those scary 'farmyard experiences' that Mum tortured us with when me and Pete were little. But my feeling that I'd stumbled onto the set of a horror movie intensified when I turned to see two black figures racing towards me brandishing gardening implements.

'Hi, Chris,' said Ariel, planting her spade in the ground. 'I didn't actually think you'd come, but I'm really glad that you did.' She stepped forward like she was about to hug me, but thankfully thought better of it when she saw her dirty hands. 'This is my mum, Penny.'

Without wanting to sound like a quote from that book of chat-up lines we found in your dad's garage, it really was quite hard to tell mother and daughter apart: both wore jeans and a plain black hoodie, both sported the same scarecrow hair-do and, instead of makeup, they were both plastered with mud.

'Hello, Chris,' said Penny, taking my hand and giving it an agonising squeeze. 'Welcome to *Honesty*.'

'It's what we call this place,' explained Ariel. '*Honesty Smallholdings*.'

'Before we go any further, I need to tell you how sad I was about Declan,' said Penny. 'I lost *my* best friend to breast cancer a few years back. The pain never goes completely, but it does get better, I promise.'

Honesty might have been ready to welcome *me*; unfortunately I didn't feel quite the same way about honesty. Penny must have sensed as much.

'Why don't you take Chris for a walk round the lake? They say the heron's back.'

'Come on,' said Ariel. 'It's this way.' We were just

heading towards the reed beds when she noticed my soggy trainers. 'You're not wearing those, are you?'

It must have been the first time she'd laughed at someone else's clothing and not the other way around.

Ariel would have made a good TV presenter, even though she'd already told me that she and her mum didn't have a telly. All I could see were reeds and murky water, but she did a twenty-minute song and dance routine every time she spotted the occasional starling or a distant duck.

'I suppose you'll tell everyone at school what a weirdo I am,' she said as we made our way towards the hut on the other side of the water. 'Sorry, I . . . I didn't think . . . I mean, you couldn't, could you? I was just . . .'

I smiled in an effort to reassure her.

Ariel laughed. She *did* have a sense of humour after all. '*I* thought it was weird too. When Mum told me we were going to give away all our possessions and live without money in the middle of nowhere, I thought she was off her head.'

Ariel really *did* have a sense of humour.

'That's what Declan thought,' she said, reading my mind like one of her paperbacks, 'but it's true. We're eighty-five per cent self-sufficient. They give us the plot rent-free in exchange for volunteer work on the nature reserve. And any other stuff we need, we get from bartering our produce.'

I was a little uncomfortable that she'd sneaked your name into the monologue. So I was glad when we reached the hut and she pushed open the door. 'Shhh,' she said, rather unnecessarily. 'We don't want to scare anything.'

The bird hide looked out onto the reed beds through a long, narrow window, which was open to the elements. Completely barren, apart from a whiteboard where you could write down everything you'd spotted that day, a long wooden bench and an old bloke on the end with a thermos flask and telephoto lens.

'That's Reg,' she whispered, waving at the man with the camera and leading me to the other end of the bench. 'He's snapped more birds than the paparazzi.'

And *now* she was making – borderline sexist – jokes.

We stared in library silence at the still, grey water, until suddenly Reg's camera started clicking so ferociously I thought Simon Cowell and the entire royal family must have swum past. 'Oh my word,' he wheezed. 'She's back.'

'Down there,' whispered Ariel, pointing at a grey streak in the rushes. 'It's a heron. Isn't she beautiful?'

I wasn't so sure. The long-necked creature wading clumsily through the shallow water was hardly the Angelina of the animal kingdom. (She wasn't even the Charlize Heron!)

'Here, take these,' said Ariel, pulling a pair of minia-ture binoculars from her hoodie pocket and hanging the cord around my neck. 'Use the wheel in the middle to focus.'

Its white, showgirl feathers at the front were pretty hazy, but as I ran my way up the black tramlines on the heron's neck, everything became clearer.

Because that's when I saw what it had in its beak.

'Declan would have loved this,' sighed Ariel.

It was a huge rat. Almost as big as the one the cat brought in that nearly gave Dad a heart attack.

'He said nature was nearly as cool as comedy.'

The rat twisted and kicked, vainly attempting to free himself from the powerful yellow beak.

'I really miss him,' sniffed Ariel. 'He was pretty special, wasn't he?'

The heron was dunking her victim under the water. Every time the rodent emerged, he twitched a little less violently, looked a little more like a drowned rat.

'But you know that better than anyone, don't you?' said Ariel, gently squeezing my shoulder. 'It's worse for you, of course it is. Is that why you can't . . .?'

The heron squeezed a little tighter. The rat twitched for the very last time.

'You know what I'd really like?' said Ariel. 'I'd like it if, one day, you'd tell me everything you know about him – all his little secrets.'

It was what I wanted too. At least I thought I did. But as soon as she said it, the whole world seemed to close in on me again, just like it had in the CAMHS office, and it felt like something terrible was about to happen. The lump rising in my throat was almost as massive as the rat-shaped bulge descending in the heron's. The last thing I wanted was for Ariel to see me cry.

'Steady on,' said Reg, as I stumbled to the door, sending his thermos tumbling.

'Chris, Chris, wait up,' shouted Ariel. 'Look I wasn't trying to . . . What's the matter with you?'

I'd calmed down a bit by the time she caught up with me.

'I'm so sorry,' she said, hugging herself through her hoodie pocket. 'I thought maybe talking about him would be good for you.'

So did the professionals, but it didn't mean they were right.

'Please don't go,' she said, as I searched anxiously for the way out. 'There's something else we could do – something that might help.'

The prospect of Monopoly with Dad was enough to make me hesitate.

'I promise I won't talk,' said Ariel. 'Come on, follow me.'

She led me across the wooden walkways until we came to a lumpy patch of ground dotted with weeds. 'Double digging,' she said, reversing a wheelbarrow out of the tool shed. 'Mum wants to plant broad beans here, so we need to let the earth breathe.' She returned to the shed for two spades and a garden fork. 'Here, take this. I know it sounds crazy, but digging's probably the best way I know of chilling out. Come on, I'll show you.'

As you probably remember from that DT project where we were supposed to make spice racks and mine turned out like a lump of wood with three nails in, I'm not that great with tools. In fact, if ever I pick up a screwdriver, my dad says I look like a 'cow with a calculator'.

Even so, it was much easier than listening to Ariel. I was glistening with sweat and my back was killing me, but there was a definite satisfaction in digging a trench, mixing in a layer of compost and then filling it again with the earth from the next one. We worked steadily for almost an hour. And as the setting sun turned the lake into an orangey paradise that would have looked great on a postcard in the gift shop, I actually started believing that things could only get better.

'Ariel! Ariel!' called her mum. 'Hurry up, it's time.'

Ariel stopped digging and waved back at her. 'Let's just clean up these tools and then we can have a drink.'

Penny was waiting outside the caravan with two glasses of cloudy liquid. 'Made with apples from our own orchard,' she said proudly. 'There you go, Chris. I reckon you've earned it.'

Considering how disgusting it looked, it was actually pretty delicious. And it was only after I'd polished off the last morsel of soggy apple that I saw what was lurking at the rear of the caravan, and chilling-out suddenly turned into just plain chilling.

'It's supposed to be Declan,' explained Ariel. 'We wanted to make something to remember him by. This way, it feels like he's always looking out for me. What do you think of it?'

Not for the first time, being dumb felt like a gift from the gods, because it freaked me out right from the start. The life-sized straw man peering into the back window wasn't a comedy character like the guy in *The Wizard of Oz*, he was a sad, faceless automaton who couldn't even have cracked a couple of bad jokes at his best friend's wedding.

'Anyway,' said Penny, hastily grabbing my glass. 'It's been lovely meeting you, Chris, but there's something Ariel and I have to do now.'

'Meditation,' said Ariel grimly. 'Twenty minutes at dusk and dawn.'

'She loves it really,' said Penny. 'It's the only way to tune out of all the rubbish and focus on what's really going on in your life. You should try it some time.'

It sounded about as appealing as my next session with Dr Tennant.

'Now why don't you take Chris back to the loggery while I light a candle and get the music ready?'

It was growing darker. Ariel led me through the gap

66

in the trees and out onto the main path. 'Come again before the end of the holiday,' she said. 'Maybe next time you'll be able to talk about Declan.'

I can't deny I was tempted. I'd really enjoyed Ariel's company, but her determination to talk about you left me wondering if perhaps what I really needed was a new friend; someone who didn't know the first thing about Declan Norris.

It was almost as if a malevolent Fairy Godmother was granting my every wish.

The next day after lunch, I discovered how Dad had managed to wangle so much time off work.

'He's the boss's son,' he said, somehow succeeding in looking guilty just stacking the dishwasher. 'He doesn't know anyone round here, so Dominic thought it might be rather nice for the two of you to get together. Obviously I've told him about your . . . problem.'

Mum had even popped home from work to back him up. 'I called Dr Tennant and she said it was a good idea. You might even find things easier with a complete stranger. And at least you won't end up covered in mud,' she added pointedly.

'I told you they were making more redundancies at work,' said Dad. 'This could be my chance to earn a few more brownie points. It's only for a couple of hours. You never know, you might even enjoy yourself.'

Could I have *been* more speechless?

'We'll take that as a yes, then,' said Mum, straightening the badge with her name on.

'Great,' said Dad. 'He'll be here in half an hour.'

It was the ultimate humiliation: having your parents arranging your social life for you. No, not quite. The ultimate humiliation would surely come when the boss's son realised the full implications of a new 'playmate' who was about as talkative as a Trappist monk at a sponsored silence. But I tried to stay positive. At least they'd warned him about my 'difficulties'. And the one big advantage of a complete stranger was that he wouldn't know the first thing about me and you.

It was a chance to reinvent myself, so I dashed up to my room and set about rearranging things. My uncoolest CDs were dispatched to the drawer under the bed, alongside my battered Harry Potters and the comedy DVDs that we only watched when we wanted to relive our youth. You were always saying it was unnatural for any teenager to have a bedroom as tidy as mine, so I grabbed a couple of freshly ironed shirts from the wardrobe and draped them over the back of a chair, carefully balancing my unread copy of *The Catcher in the Rye* on top.

Half an hour later, a flash sports car pulled up outside. I watched from the window as a high-heeled lady in an unseasonably short skirt climbed out. She tottered round to the other door, holding it open for my new playmate like a chauffeur.

My heart sank when I saw how cool he looked in his multi-layered ensemble of deliberately unmatching designer-labelled scruffiness. But that was nothing compared with the sheer panic that gripped me when he removed his black fedora hat and I realised who it was.

My first instinct was to make a run for it, but Dad was already at the front door doing his 'ever so humble' act. The situation was such a disaster, it was almost funny, which is probably why I giggled hysterically as the footsteps on the stairs grew louder and I scanned the tidiest teenage bedroom in history for somewhere to hide.

'*There* you are,' said Dad a few moments later. 'What were you trying to do – find Narnia?' His nervous laugh made the 'joke' even worse. 'Now come over here, Chris. You've got a visitor.'

I closed the wardrobe behind me, wondering just how long my cataclysmic run of bad luck could continue.

'You remember, Dominic, my *excellent* sales manager, don't you, Chris? Well, this is his son, Will. But apparently you two have already met.'

Will Hunt's well-chiselled features gleamed like the sun. 'That's right, Mr Hughes. Christopher and I sit next to each other in practically every lesson.'

'Well, then, you'll know that Chris is the strong, silent type,' said Dad with a playful wink. 'So I've rented you guys a couple of movies. Why don't you let the guest choose?'

'Great, thanks,' said Will, studying the cover of *Spider-Man 3* with barely hidden disgust.

Dad backed out of the door, like a butler in an award-winning costume drama. 'I'll leave you to it, then. Have a great time now.'

'Bet you didn't expect to see *me*,' said Will, checking out my DVD collection.

He was right there. Half-term was proving pretty tragic, but at least I hadn't had to put up with any more of his stupid 'dumb' jokes.

'So where's the Xbox then?'

It was downstairs. I hadn't touched it since the night of Ella's party. The *Call of Duty* was only a distant whisper now you weren't here to ward off the zombie hordes.

'OK, never mind,' he said, pacing the floor with his thumb in his mouth. 'What else have you got?'

I shrugged helpfully.

'Look, this wasn't my idea, you know, but now that I'm here, why don't we make the best of it?'

Back then I often caught myself staring gormlessly into space. I must have looked a bit like that bloke in the iron mask.

Will chuckled appreciatively. 'Love the Mr Mime act,

by the way. I thought my dyslexia thing was pretty special, but your no talking routine is totally genius.'

I was trying to figure out what he meant when the door swung open.

'Sorry, guys, have you got a minute?' Pete *never* came into my bedroom, and he certainly never apologised.

'No problem,' said Will. 'How can we help?'

'It was you I wanted to talk to actually,' said Pete, looking more like the shyest dork in the computer club than the self-proclaimed King of Year Nine. 'Gaz and me were wondering where you got your hair wax.'

'You can't buy it here I'm afraid,' said Will. 'My dad has it flown over from Italy. But I tell you what, next time we put in an order, I'll try and get you guys sorted.'

'Brilliant . . . Thanks,' said my brother, backing out of the door like a footman in an award-winning costume drama.

'Hang on a minute,' said Will. 'Do you mind if I ask you something?'

'Sure,' said Pete.

'Is this guy for real? I mean, I didn't want to ruin it for him at school, but I certainly wasn't expecting the silent treatment here too. You're his brother; it's a scam, right?'

Pete didn't need any encouragement to talk about my condition. 'That's what everyone thought to begin with. He's always been a bit weird, if you know what I mean.

It was only when they took him to a shrink that I knew he wasn't faking it.'

'And that whole story about his best mate dying; that was actually true, then? I thought they were just winding up the new kid.'

'It's true all right,' said Pete, trying not to stare too hard at his hair. 'Chris and Dec were really close. They had this whole comedy double-act thing going.'

'The truth really is stranger than fiction,' said Will thoughtfully. 'Thanks for that. And don't worry, I'll keep you posted about the hair wax. Catch you later, yeah?

'I don't blame you for being angry,' he said as Pete left. 'If I'd have known you were genuinely screwed-up, I wouldn't have made all those jokes about you. I can't help myself sometimes.

'Look, I don't want to be rude about your dad's taste in films or anything, but why don't we watch one of yours.' He selected the movie on the far right hand side of my DVD shelf and chucked it at me. 'Alphabetical order, eh? You ought to loosen up a bit.'

Yeah, all right, Declan; just because you said the same thing, doesn't mean he was right. At least I could locate season seven of *The Simpsons* in less than three hours.

'Go on, put it on,' said Will, flopping down on my bed without taking his shoes off. 'You look like you could do with a good laugh.'

At least it was better than having him talk at me for

the next two hours, so I balanced the laptop on my bedside table and drew up the Pokémon beanbag that I really should have binned at the end of primary school. I still had a bit of a soft spot for *Zoolander* too, but the harder Will laughed the more miserable I became. The trouble was, practically every line reminded me of you, Dec. We did the whole of the walk-off scene (with Luke Corcoran as David Bowie) for the war graves trip fundraiser talent show, and you spent every PE lesson in Year Eight perfecting your 'blue steel'.

Will insisted on watching the special features too. After the outtakes and the deleted scenes – which are deleted for a reason by the way – we sat in silence for nine and a half minutes (I kept track on my clock radio) until Dad came to tell us that his lift had arrived. The worst afternoon since the magician at your ninth birthday party turned out to be a mime artist was officially over. I consoled myself with the fact that a repeat performance was about as likely as Rob the Slob dropping out of university to join a rock band.

'All right, then, lads?' said Dad, hopefully. 'Have you had a good time?'

Will Hunt's smile was brighter than the August sun. 'Yeah, great thanks, Mr Hughes. We should do it again sometime.'

* * *

That night when I raided the fridge, I overheard Mum and Dad through the serving hatch.

'Are you sure about this, Trevor? We don't really know anything about the boy.'

'What's there to know?' said Dad. 'Just that he's had a bit of a rough ride lately, and Dominic doesn't want him to get in with the wrong crowd. *I* think we should encourage it.'

'What was he like, anyway?'

'Very polite,' said Dad. 'A hell of a lot better than our two.'

'And what about Chris? Did he take to him, do you think?'

'How the hell should I know?' said Dad. 'He was difficult enough to read when he was talking. He could be a budding serial killer for all I know.'

'That's not funny, Trevor.'

'It's starting to get to me, that's all. I mean, how is it he can come up with a whole essay on symbolism in *The Crucible*, but the moment you ask him what's going on in that head of his, he can't even write a simple sentence? You heard what that shrink woman said: she's never seen anything like it.'

'Dr Tennant said it was very unusual,' snapped Mum. 'Apparently mutism *can* be caused by a trauma, but it's rare for it to last this long.' She was sounding like an expert already; it was just the same when Pete developed that allergy thing. 'Anyway, stop having a go at Christopher. He's not doing it just to irritate you, you know. The poor boy really *can't* talk.'

'Sorry, sorry, I just want to make him better.'

'Well, maybe this isn't the way,' said Mum. 'Couldn't you put him off or something?'

'I *can't*,' said Dad. 'Dominic was over the moon when he called; said it was the chirpiest he'd seen Will for months.'

'What's more important to you, Trevor: keeping your job or your own son's happiness?'

'I'd say the two are inextricably linked, wouldn't you?' said Dad.

It was Mum who broke the heavy silence. 'What are we going to tell Chris?'

'Nothing,' said Dad. 'Well, not yet, anyway. Let's wait until it's written in blood.'

Dad was getting good at this surveillance lark. It was like that game we played at nursery – you remember, What's the Time, Mr Wolf? Whenever I swung round to catch him out, he seemed to vanish into thin air, leaving only the faintest suspicion that I was being followed.

It was the Friday of half-term. I'd lived in fear that Will Hunt would reappear on my doorstep, but it looked like I'd avoided another charity matinee with the boss's son. Even so, when Dad disappeared upstairs for his video conference, I decided to make absolutely sure.

There was someone I *did* want to see. Don't get me wrong, Declan, I didn't fancy her or anything. I still thought of Ariel as *your* girlfriend and I would never have let my feelings run away with me like that. But it was complicated. How was it possible to be excited about seeing someone and yet to be dreading it at the same time?

So I felt a mixture of disappointment *and* relief when, apart from the pesky chickens, *Honesty Smallholdings* appeared to be completely deserted. I was turning to leave when I spotted smoke coming from the caravan. Like that song Dad kept playing when he wanted to prove he had 'cool taste in music', I couldn't decide whether to stay or go. And there was a rat-sized lump in my throat as I knocked three times on the door.

'Chris,' said Ariel, fanning away the steam with her paperback. 'You'd better come in. I was just thinking about you.'

The red velvet curtains made it seem like something from a fairy tale, and I couldn't believe how tiny it was inside – just a padded seat under the window with a fold-away table in front, a kitchen area with a tiny sink, and finally what I assumed to be the living space, comprising two ancient armchairs that looked like refugees from an old people's home and a jam-packed bookcase.

At least it was warm. That was down to the wood-burning stove in the corner with the witch's cauldron bubbling away on top.

'Sorry about the smell,' said Ariel. 'I've been boiling up some beech nuts for our homemade detergent.'

I hate to say it, mate, but the thought of a straw Declan peering through the window twenty-four/seven was really doing my head in. So was some of the artwork hanging from the ceiling.

'How do you like my dreamcatcher?' said Ariel.

The willow hoop was decorated with a few skanky feathers, a photograph of a man in a blue suit, some nail varnish, two cinema tickets and a cuddly puppy thing with a yellow nose. Knowing Ariel it probably represented something – the loss of innocence, perhaps?

'The web in the middle is supposed to catch bad dreams,' she said, lifting the pot off the stove and draining the contents into a sieve in the sink, 'but it doesn't seem to be doing much good lately.'

I knew how she felt.

'Mum's planting some new reed beds. She wants me to count the nesting boxes in the wood. Feel like helping out?'

I'm sure grandmama had warned me about going into the woods with strange girls, but I smiled and nodded all the same.

The woodland behind the caravan seemed to go on

for miles. Ariel said that if you planted trees close together they grew up straight and tall as they reached for the light. It also meant it was kind of gloomy in there, and although I tried to concentrate as she identified the different species, I couldn't help thinking that if Ariel did a runner, I'd probably be wandering round in circles until I dropped dead of exhaustion.

'What's the matter?' she said. 'You seem a bit jumpy.'

I had a funny feeling he was still following me. If Dad popped out from behind a tree, I'd probably drop dead of embarrassment.

'See that really big box on the copper beech?' said Ariel. 'We had a pair of barn owls last year.'

It felt uncomfortable to begin with; letting her lead me deeper into the woods like that. Who knows what difficult questions she might bombard me with. But after thirty-seven nesting boxes, I was starting to chill out. The woody smell reminded me of Mum's relaxing bath gel, and anyway, there was something about Ariel that really made you want to open up to her. Not that I knew what I wanted to open up about; just that it was something really bad.

'That's the lot,' she said, ticking the last one off in her notebook. 'We can go back now. I'm glad it's a bit of a trek, because there's something I want to talk to you about.'

It looked like the interrogation was about to begin. She picked up a beech twig and swished it through the damp leaves. 'Declan said you were the funniest person he'd ever met.'

Out on the lakeshore, a redshank whistled sarcastically.

'You even told him his first joke.'

Q: What did the traffic light say to the car? A: Don't look now, I'm changing.

'I was actually quite jealous. I think that's why he wanted us to be friends.'

It was the second time she'd said it. I was starting to believe it might even be true.

'That's why I want to help you, Chris. I mean, you don't want to be like this forever, do you?'

A few weeks before, I couldn't have returned her concerned gaze. This time, I even managed to shake my head.

Ariel dropped the beech twig and took my hand. 'Sometimes it really gets to me. If I'd just . . . *insisted* he walked home with me and Mum, everything would be so different – do you know what I mean?'

High above us, a jay chattered a tuneless warning.

'What *is* it, Chris? What is it that's eating *you*?' Her eyes burned into me, like an ace interrogator's. 'You can tell me, you know. I'm your friend. It's something to do with Declan, isn't it?'

And suddenly I knew that the answer was yes.

'Come on, Chris, you can do this. I know you can.'

That's right, Dec; it had taken me a while get there,

but as Mr Catchpole would have been delighted to discover, I could finally 'see the wood for the trees'. Suddenly I knew exactly what it meant, that terrible feeling in the CAMHS office. There were even words in the back of my head to explain it.

It was bad, very bad. And once I managed to say it out loud, things would never be the same again. Yes, I know, mate, it was totally dumb of me trying to talk, but Ariel was squeezing my hand and staring expectantly into my eyes. I could do it. I knew I could.

And yet, when I opened my mouth, all that came out was a shrill scream, loud enough to wake the dead. It didn't sound like my voice at all. Perhaps that's what happened if you didn't speak for six weeks. It was only when I saw the terror in her eyes that I realised it was Ariel's.

'Behind you,' she said, pointing into the shadows.

And then I saw it too: the white, skeletal figure in the long black trench coat, its eyeless sockets oozing blood, that was slowly advancing on us with outstretched arms.

'Go away,' said Ariel defiantly. 'There's nothing for you here. If you come back to the caravan we might sort you out something to eat.'

The sound of muffled laughter turned into a full-throated roar when the skeleton ripped off its mask. 'Trick or treat?' said Will Hunt, his jubilant smile lighting up the forest. 'Oh my God, you two, you should see your faces!'

Ariel let go of my hand. 'What are *you* doing here?'

'Trying to catch up with Christopher,' said Will, his shoulders still shaking with mirth. 'What have you been doing to the poor guy? He looks like he's about to cry or something.'

'I've been trying to help him,' said Ariel. 'He was going to say something, I know he was. And then you went and ruined it all with your childish play acting.'

'If you say so,' said Will. 'Although if you ask me, he doesn't exactly look like he's dying for a chat.'

'Tell him, Chris,' said Ariel.

This time I couldn't even look at her feet.

'See what I mean?' said Will. 'And, anyway, I thought you liked plays.'

'And I thought *you* were grounded,' said Ariel.

'I am,' said Will, 'but my dad thinks Christopher here will be a "good influence". In fact, he's so keen for us to be friends that he actually got his PA to call the taxi himself.'

Ariel's small white hand formed a small white fist. 'Maybe it would be better if you waited until Chris was . . . well, a bit more like his old self. He's been through a lot lately.'

Will shrugged. 'If that's what he wants, fine.'

I tried desperately to focus on their conversation, but all I could think about was the shocking discovery that had just shattered my world. I couldn't believe I'd tried to blurt it out like that.

'Oh, by the way, that's quite a little commune you've got going,' said Will. 'Holly's into all that self-sufficiency stuff.'

'Who's Holly?' said Ariel. 'Your mum?'

'She's *not* my mother,' said Will. 'She's just a fourth-rate catalogue model who got lucky.'

'Yes, well, we're heading back to *Honesty* now,' said Ariel, 'so you'd better tag along. And you can tell your . . . friend, Holly, that me and Mum have managed to live completely without money for the last eighteen months.'

Will Hunt was absent-mindedly poking his index finger through the eye-socket of his Halloween mask. 'My dad always says that money makes the world go round.'

'Money is the root of all evil,' said Ariel, blushing slightly as she played with her hair.

'Try telling me that the next time you have to fly cattle class,' said Will, smiling.

'We don't fly at all any more,' said Ariel. 'Mum said she had a carbon footprint the size of an elephant's.'

'Let's hope she hasn't got a butt to match,' whispered Will, almost making me laugh for the first time since the accident.

The sun was setting. A blackbird chirped its early evening melody. At least my new secret was safe for a while, but I had a feeling that if I spent much more time with Ariel, there was a distinct possibility that she'd get me to sing.

'Come on,' she said, with a disappointed smile. 'It's this way.'

'This is delicious,' said Will. 'Are the apples from your own orchard?'

Penny was feeding the chickens. I tried to keep very still as they clucked around my feet. 'That's right,' she said. 'Everything tastes so much better when you've grown it yourself.'

'They're solar panels, aren't they?' said Will, pointing up at the shiny, plastic mirror suspended above the caravan. 'I'm impressed.'

'We're completely off-grid here,' said Penny, stooping down to greet her favourite cockerel. 'It's very liberating.'

'I bet it is,' said Will, dumping his apple juice in the long grass while her back was turned. 'I was just telling these guys that my stepmother, Holly, is a bit of an eco-warrior. In fact, she's even going to chain herself to a tree or something at the new superstore protest.'

'Then I'll probably see her there,' said Penny.

Will was already admiring the straw figure at the rear of the caravan. 'This is amazing. I really like the way it seems to be watching you.'

That's what I hated about it. It was almost as if your stupid statue could read my mind.

Penny threw down her last handful of chicken feed. 'We created it in memory of Declan. He was Chris's best friend – and Ariel's boyfriend, of course.'

'Oh *really*,' said Will. 'I didn't know that.'

You could almost hear Ariel's teeth grinding. 'Isn't it about time we got started, Mum?' She turned to me and Will. 'You'll have to go, I'm afraid. We need to meditate.'

'Right, fine,' said Will with a turbo-charged smile. 'I'll walk Christopher back to the loggery. I want a quick word with him, anyway – bye now.'

Ariel grabbed my hand as I started to follow. 'This isn't over, Chris. You wanted to talk about Declan, I *know* you did. Maybe it's too soon right now, but whenever you're ready, I'll be here for you, I promise.' She dug her fingernails into my palm. 'And if you take my advice, you'll steer well clear of Will Hunt. I mean, it didn't take the others long to suss him out, did it? You might be a good influence on *him*, but I have a feeling it wouldn't work both ways.'

I had a feeling she was probably right. Will's popularity rating had plummeted dramatically since his first day. All the same it didn't stop me reclaiming my hand and hurrying after him.

'Lovely to meet you, Will,' called Penny. 'See you again sometime.'

'Well, I hope for their sake they've got decent health

insurance,' whispered Will, as we disappeared into the trees. 'Did you *see* all that chicken poo?'

Back at the beetle loggery, he turned serious for once. 'Look, it's none of my business or anything, it's just that I couldn't help noticing how miserable you looked back there. Now, I'm sure Ariel is a really nice person. And there's a time and a place for the touchy feely stuff – of course there is. But if you ask me, what you really need right now is a bloody good laugh.'

A few days earlier, the prospect of a sleepover at Will Hunt's house would have been about as enticing as a walking holiday in the Lake District with Rob the Slob. I was still angry with Dad for arranging it all behind my back, but after the revelation in the forest, I was so desperate for any form of distraction that I silenced my misgivings and threw my rucksack into the back of the car. It would be a relief to get away from Mum for a few hours. She was doing my head in with her over-attentive parenting routine. In fact 'a bloody good laugh' was probably just what the psychiatrist ordered.

'It's a beautiful house,' said Dad, trying to sound optimistic and failing miserably. 'Very modern design – ninety per cent glass. Your mother and I were there three Christmases ago for Dominic's drinks party. Don't you remember, Pauline? There was that fantastic jazz band?'

'I remember some sweaty person trying to sell me accidental death insurance,' said Mum. 'And the food wasn't that great, either.'

'It's a wonderful location anyway,' said Dad. 'Some people would kill for a view like that.'

'Dominic, for instance,' said Mum.

'Dominic's a pussycat,' said Dad unconvincingly. 'You should have seen how thrilled he was that Chris and Will hit it off so well.'

Mum was a bit tearful as the electric gates slid slowly apart. 'Now you are sure about this, aren't you, Christopher?'

It couldn't possibly be any worse than sitting in my bedroom, brooding on the past. So I nodded and braced myself.

The sound of Dad's car disappearing down the long driveway saw my last chance to change my mind disappearing with it. Mum said they'd come and get me in the middle of the night if I texted them, but I knew Dad would talk her out of it. She'd even made me some special sleepover cards with such useful phrases as: *Thank you, Mrs Hunt, that was delicious, Could you direct me to the bathroom, please, Mrs Hunt?* and *Sorry, Mrs Hunt, I don't eat scrambled eggs.* But they were obviously too formal for the woman in the tight leggings and curvy top.

'Call me Holly, darling,' she said, squeezing the life out of an inflatable mattress and trying to roll it into a tight ball. 'It's all right, I know you can't actually . . . Dom told me about your little problem.'

Dressed like that, she was much more of a Holly than a Mrs Hunt, anyway.

'Will . . . Will, hurry up,' she shouted. 'Your friend's here.'

The downstairs living space had more sofas than a dentist's waiting room and a whole art gallery of canvases that looked like refugees from the Tate Modern. The view of the Downs might well have been spectacular in daylight; all you could see now was a dense black hole that reminded me of my life.

'Look, I'm sure you'll be all right,' said Holly, suddenly sounding serious for a minute, 'but you won't let him talk you into anything . . . silly, will you? Will can get a bit . . .' She smiled sympathetically. '*Anyway*, Kasia's in the annex if you need something, and Dominic's promised to be home by midnight so you'll probably be fine. Could you sit on that for me, darling? It's got a life of its own.'

I sat on her bulging suitcase while she fastened the lock.

'Thanks, pet. We're setting up camp before the bulldozers move in. The last thing that town needs is another superstore.' She checked her face in the shiny black coffee table. 'There are plenty of rooms, of course, but I've told Kasia to make up the spare bed next to

Will's. I'm sure you don't want to be on your own, and *he*'s used to it from school.'

I showed her my *Thank you very much, Mrs Hunt* card, thinking that if I'd been able to say it out loud, my tone of voice would definitely have conveyed that I had my doubts.

'It's Holly, darling, I told you. Now, I think you'd better go upstairs and find his room. It's down the corridor, turn left, and then it's third on the right. You can't miss it – it stinks of adolescent boy.'

I left Holly cackling into the coffee table and headed slowly upstairs. I'm not sure about the stench of adolescence, but the sound of gunshots and screaming coming from Will Hunt's bedroom was a real blast from the past. It reminded me of you, Declan – all those hours we'd spent on the Xbox together. How could I even think of having a laugh with anyone else? And for a moment I felt like turning round and making a run for it. It was only when I remembered what I'd tried to blab to Ariel that I made a fist and knocked.

'Come in!'

He was sitting in a black swivel chair, controller thumbs twitching, staring up at the scenes of carnage on the mini cinema screen on the wall. I almost expected him to turn round and say something like, 'So, Mr Bond, we meet again,' but he was much more interested in shooting-up tourists at the airport. 'Have a seat,' he said, blasting the guy in duty free with his Kalashnikov. 'God, I love this level. Talk about adrenalin rush.'

I perched on the edge of the white leather sofa. The body count mounted.

'Why don't you have a go?' said Will, handing me a spare controller. 'We'll play it together if you like.'

At first I felt kind of guilty; you were really the shoot 'em up specialist, weren't you, Dec? But as soon as we got out of the lift and started mowing down innocent civilians, I began to relax.

'Go on,' said Will. 'Just go mental.'

We rampaged through the departure lounge, firing randomly. And by the time Holly popped her head round the door to say goodbye, I was totally getting into it.

'Kasia will bring up the pizzas when you're ready,' she said, 'and you will look after Chris, won't you, William?'

'You can count on it,' he murmured, decimating a row of recently orphaned luggage.

'And remember poor Rupert,' said Holly. 'I don't know what's got into him lately.'

Will stood at the top of the escalator and picked off the last survivors. 'Yeah . . . right.'

'I'll be off then,' said Holly, averting her eyes from the bloodshed as she backed out of the door. 'Those trees won't save themselves, you know.'

'Methinks the lady doth protest too much,' muttered Will.

I had a feeling it was supposed to be a joke, but don't ask me to explain it, Declan.

Our killing spree continued for the next half hour. In the end, it was Will who laid down his controller. 'Let's eat, shall we? I'm sure you're starving, and there's plenty of time to get to know each other. I'll text Kasia with our orders. Now what's your tipple? Let me guess, Orangina? Diet Coke?'

I don't know if they were from some posh new take-away or Kasia the housekeeper cooked them herself, but they were the best pizzas I've ever tasted. You would definitely have approved of the crisp, thin crust, the generous layer of mozzarella and delicately spiced pepperoni. You see, Dec, that was another thing you two had in common: pepperoni was *his* favourite flavour too! And, just for a millisecond, it was almost like old times.

But as soon as I'd burped my way through half a litre of Diet Coke and teased out the last morsel of Chunky Monkey ice cream with a long, silver spoon, my mood took a turn for the worse. The massacre at the airport had taken my mind off it for a while but after all that burping and pepperoni, it was only natural that I should start thinking about you again. And it wasn't a warm fuzzy feeling. It was a bleak, kick in the guts kind of feeling that I would have done almost anything to avoid.

'Right,' said Will. 'I can see you need another adrenalin boost. Let's go and have some fun with Rupert.'

He led me downstairs and out through the front door. A new set of security lights clicked on every time we passed a different feature. Just beyond the maze and the tennis courts we came to a halt outside a building that looked remarkably like the luxury log cabin we'd stayed in when we went to Cornwall.

'He's in the shed,' said Will, pushing the door open and calling into the gloom. 'Oh Rupert, there's someone here who wants to meet you.'

I didn't see him at first. The smell reminded me of that pet shop on the Brighton Road, and I had my work cut out just trying not to puke. It was only when I looked into the far corner that I saw his little white face pressed up against the bars.

'He was supposed to be some sort of surrogate friend,' said Will, selecting a cardboard box from the shelf and cautiously approaching the cage. 'They meant well, I suppose. But I'm fifteen years old, for heaven's sake. I choose my own friends, don't I, Rupert?'

It was slightly disturbing to see him talking to an animal like that, but I had every sympathy with the choosing your own friends part, and, stupid though it may sound, I was just a tiny bit relieved that Rupert had turned out to be a rabbit.

'Apparently being capable of caring for an animal is a sign of maturity,' said Will, 'but to be honest, I don't even like him that much.'

The feeling was obviously mutual. Rupert snarled as Will grabbed hold of his hind legs and squashed and squeezed him into the cardboard box before hastily closing the lid.

'Right, let's go back inside. There's something I really want to show you.'

Without Will, it would have been so easy to get lost. The lower ground floor was a warren of thickly carpeted corridors that all looked the same. But it was the smell of chlorine, that grew stronger as we reached the tiled area with the sauna and exercise machines, which really set me panicking. It reminded me of my weekly drowning lessons in Year Four. By the sound of his frenzied attempts to burrow out of the box, I'd have said that Rupert felt exactly the same.

'You are *so* going to love this,' said Will, almost running through the changing area and stepping out onto the side of a kidney-shaped swimming pool that was bigger than the one at our hotel in Barcelona. 'Like I said, Christopher, what you really need is a bloody good laugh.'

It didn't take a two-page questionnaire to establish that Rupert was one extremely stressed pet. He was kicking like crazy when Will magicked him from the box and dangled his back paws into the water.

'If he sinks he's just a cute little wabbit,' giggled Will, struggling to keep hold of his furry prisoner. 'If he swims, he's a *witch*.'

Even if I'd been able to speak up on poor Rupert's behalf, I don't think Will would have listened. He'd already started the countdown in a (really good) American accent. *'Ten, nine* . . . What a laugh, eh? . . . *Eight, seven, six* . . . Told you we'd have some fun, didn't I? . . . *Five, four, three, two* . . .'

Part of me was horrified; part of me really wanted to see what happened next.

'We have lift off!' yelled Will, launching Rupert head first into the deep end with a squeal of delight.

He can't have been underwater for more than a few seconds, but it seemed like several hours.

'Looks like he's just a cute little bunny wabbit after all.' Will grinned, grabbing his mobile and filming the whole thing in high-definition.

I must have been holding my breath for as long as Rupert. The air flooded back into my lungs when a little white head appeared at the foot of the slide.

'What were you expecting, anyway?' said Will. 'I always knew he was a witch.'

And to begin with, I have to admit it *was* pretty hilarious. Rupert swam a series of kidney-shaped circuits, head arched in a futile attempt to keep it out of the water, legs bicycling furiously. The problem was, he couldn't find anywhere to get out. Although a trained rabbit might just have negotiated the ladder at the deep end, there was no way he could pull himself out of the water with those tiny front paws. Sooner or later he'd be too tired to stay afloat.

'That'll teach him to try and bite me,' said Will, as Rupert started running out of steam, like the non-Duracell bunny. 'Face it, Bugsy – you're going down!'

You would definitely have found the next bit funny, Declan – Will certainly did. Because there was nothing for it but to fling myself fully-clothed into the water and doggy-paddle after the petrified rabbit like a hydrophobic greyhound.

Will's bedroom was now humming with the great smell of adolescence. The damp clothes that I'd draped across the state-of-the-art heated towel rail/mirror in the ensuite bathroom were steaming nicely, creating a subtle blend of stale sweat, chlorine, that deodorant that's supposed to make you irresistible to women and the merest hint of warm blood from where Rupert had scratched me when I rescued him.

If it hadn't been for my brother, I might have found it slightly unnerving. As it was, the fact that Will had been in the bathroom for nearly an hour didn't bother me, and I was actually starting to calm down. Luxuriating in the double bed with the memory foam mattress and two plump pillows, I could check out Will's posters, his taste in music and his extensive collection of Blu-rays. The devices to play them on might have been smaller, better and with more memory, but it was the usual mixture of flavour-of-the-month indie boys, movies about killing, a couple of dead legends and a Banksy poster. Apart from a few omissions in the comedy department, he had pretty much the same sort of stuff as you or me.

'I wouldn't have let him drown, you know,' said Will, emerging from the bathroom, preceded by an invisible cloud of expensive aftershave. 'They got rid of my mother easily enough. Why would I give them an excuse to get rid of me? Anyway, I was only trying to cheer you up.'

I checked out the photo on the windowsill. Will and a floppy-haired accomplice were eating doughnuts in front of the Taj Mahal.

'That's my old mate, Simon,' said Will, climbing into the even larger double bed to my left and placing his mobile on the table between us. 'Si's just about the funnest guy you're ever likely to meet.'

It was one of those new words that turned Mum and Dad into born again grammar Nazis.

'Goodnight, then,' said Will. 'If it gets too stuffy in here, feel free to open a window. Oh, by the way, I hope you're not scared of the dark!'

I didn't *think* I was, but when Will killed the lights, I felt forced to reconsider. This was no ordinary darkness; it was a darkness so thick and impenetrable you could nearly taste it – and it wasn't very appetising. The silence was almost worse; not even a solitary blackbird or a predatory fox, just a faint crackle from the heated towel rail and the rise and fall of my hyperventilating.

It was a miracle that I even managed to shut my eyes, but the bizarre exercise in animal rescue must have left me so exhausted that I eventually stumbled into a fitful sleep. And that's where you come in again, Dec. Thank goodness I couldn't speak. Dr Tennant would have had a field day if I'd been able to tell her about my recurring dream.

The first bit was always pretty enjoyable. It's our debut at the Edinburgh Festival, we're top of the bill and there's a *Sold Out* sign in the foyer. And I'm waiting in the wings, quivering with excitement when the compere – who's either Principal Skinner or Joey from *Friends* – gives us the big build up.

'Now put your hands together for two of the funniest guys on the planet. Ladies and gentleman, it's Hughes and Norris.'

Oh all right, Declan, if you're going to get huffy about it again: *'It's Norris and Hughes'.*

And that's when it all goes pear-shaped. The moment I get on stage, I realise I've forgotten the first gag. And I'm half expecting you to bail me out when I look across and find that you've completely vanished. But it gets worse. My trousers have fallen down – and no one laughs. All it does is set off the heckler in the front row. So I'm wracking my brains for a clever put-down when I squint out at the audience and discover to my horror that the heckler is *you*. And you won't shut up.

'Oh look, it's the funny, funny, funny man. Come on, Mr Funny Man, say something funny. Come on, Mr Funny Man – knock 'em dead!'

I usually tried to improvise a comedy dance routine, but that night the heckler was joined by another voice. 'Wake up, wake up, you idiot, or you'll miss all the fun.'

And then someone in the audience started slapping me round the face with a wet fish. 'Come on, Christopher. Wakey, wakey!'

Will's breath stank of Chunky Monkey and mozzarella, shrouded in peppermint. His mobile was emitting a high-pitched alarm and glowing gently in the darkness. 'I'll put it on speaker phone,' he said, tapping the touch screen and then retreating slightly as if he was lighting a firework. 'That way we can both enjoy it.'

Three times it went through to voice messaging: 'Hello. You've reached Pippa Mackenzie-Brook's answering service. If it's school business, you should contact my PA during office hours. Otherwise, you can leave a message after the tone.'

The fourth time she picked up. 'You do realise it's three o' clock in the morning? This had better be important.'

And here's another thing, Declan: he was brilliant at accents too. I'm not saying Will could have convinced everyone at work experience that he was a South African exchange student like you did, but his impression of the guy who does the movie trailers was spot-on. He could even do the heavy breathing.

Pippa Mackenzie-Brooks didn't sound quite so authoritative now. 'Look . . . who is this, please?'

Will smiled, inhaling noisily, like an asthmatic, chain-smoker at the end of a fun run.

'And what do you want?'

'I'm in your kitchen,' said Will in deep, rasping American.

'You're . . . *what*?'

'I'm in your fridge,' he whispered.

'What are you talking about?'

By this time, Will was paralytic with mirth. 'So don't be surprised if you come downstairs and all the milk is gone.'

'Who is this?'

'The milk monster,' said Will, breaking the golden rule of never wetting yourself at your own jokes. 'Have you been good . . . *Pippa*?'

Miss Mackenzie-Brook's voice was regaining its authority. 'Look, this is *not* funny. I have far better things to do with my time than listen to this drivel.'

Will's voice was fast losing its American accent. 'Hey, Brooksie, my friend Christopher wants a word with you.'

It's hard to explain. Vocally challenged though I was, his hilarity was so infectious that I really wanted to be in on it. You had to be there, Declan, but when I took a deep breath and let out a loud raspberry, just for a second, it felt like my best joke ever.

Will must have thought so too, because he held up his hand so we could exchange a celebratory high five. 'Hey, Brooksie,' he said. 'There's just one more thing . . .'

But Miss Mackenzie-Brooks was long gone. Will's phone gleamed for an instant, and then it was pitch black once more.

The laughter in his voice went out with the light. 'Listen, Christopher, I've got a confession to make.'

He was starting to sound like a politician again.

'You know how I told everyone I was expelled from my old school? Actually, it didn't quite happen like that.'

Rob the Slob was already casting aspersions on his cyber-terrorist credentials.

'If you really want to know, I left because I was unhappy. Long story, but basically, I didn't cope very well when my mum and dad split up.'

I'd seen his attempts at a simple spreadsheet. This was a lot more plausible than the computer hacking scenario.

'That's why I've got a good idea of how you're feeling right now. That's why I want to give you a bit of advice.'

Accepting advice from Will Hunt felt rather like accepting lifts from strangers. All the same, I was still listening.

'I don't know what it's like for you, but I used to get really sick of people wanting to rake over my life history.'

My sessions with Dr Tennant had turned into a series of awkward silences; rather like the collected works of that playwright Mrs Woolf was always raving about.

'I mean, what's the point of wallowing in the past? You can't change anything, and it only makes you feel worse.'

I'd been re-visiting the past a lot lately. And he was right – my frequent flights of time travel were turning me into a puffy-eyed insomniac. Every few hours, a tsunami of guilt would flood over me, leaving me more depressed than ever.

'But I'll tell you what did help, shall I? It wasn't talking and it certainly wasn't Miss Mackenzie-Brooks's happiness and well-being policy.'

Was it a shiver of fear or a quiver of excitement that fizzed up my spine?

'It's dead simple. If you really want to forget all the bad stuff, you need to go a little crazy now and then. Start having some serious fun.'

I had a feeling that Will's idea of serious fun proba-bly involved more than pizza and a movie.

'I could help you if you like. Well, you know what they say, Christopher: "When the pupil is ready, the guru appears".'

How about when one door closes, all the others shut?

'We've had a good laugh tonight, haven't we? And there's plenty of fun stuff we could get up to at school.

It's your call, Christopher. But I saw how unhappy you looked up at Ariel's place. Surely it's worth giving it a try.'

The funny thing is, he was almost starting to make sense.

Eight Weeks
After The Crash

You've got to believe me, Dec; all this stuff I've been telling you, even that thing with the rabbit, it really happened, I swear. I could be mistaken about a few minor details (maybe it was a robin not a blackbird; and Holly Hunt didn't exactly cackle, she had rather a gentle laugh), but basically, it's all true.

I'm trying to show that although what I did was stupid, dangerous and occasionally illegal, if you go through the story step-by-step, it does kind of make sense. So if the next little bit sounds like something from a straight-to-DVD sci-fi movie, I want to reassure you that I most emphatically did *not* make it up.

It was the first day back after half-term. I got to my tutor base early, kind of hoping to avoid Will Hunt until our first timetabled encounter in PE. Rob the Slob always arrived at the crack of dawn. He liked to run through his official engagements in the page-a-day diary he lugged around with him like a prehistoric iPhone. Luke Corcoran only turned up early when his dad was working nights. The days of the 'Get Chris to talk' game were long gone, so they both ignored me as I sloped over to a radiator and started warming my hands.

I'm not denying that I was still reeling from my recent discovery in the wetlands, and it's true that later on I did sort of start seeing stuff, but I promise you, Declan, I know what I heard. Unbelievable though it might sound, Rob the Slob and Luke Corcoran were actually discussing theology.

'So do you believe in God then, Slobber?'

Rob the Slob was underlining in red biro. 'Depends what you mean by God.'

'You know, geezer who made the world, wrote the Bible and that?'

'I believe in order,' said Rob the Slob, saving his place with a post-it note. 'That everything happens for a reason.'

Luke Corcoran blew a thoughtful bubble. 'Yeah, but if he's, like, such a great bloke and that, why's the world so full of crap?'

Underneath his buttoned-up exterior, Rob the Slob was actually quite a humorist. 'I thought we covered all this in RE, Luke. Surely you remember Mr Willcock's fascinating lesson on free will.'

'Yeah, nice one, Slobber – you're the man.' But Luke Corcoran was in no mood to be fobbed off with cheap jokes. 'But how come you're *you* and I'm . . . me?'

'Eh?'

'Well, it's not fair, is it?' said Luke. 'Kids like you are born lucky. I've spent my whole life being in the wrong place at the wrong time.'

'It's not all luck,' said Rob the Slob, carefully refolding his fragrant PE kit. 'There is a certain amount of hard work involved.'

Luke Corcoran was cramming a lifetime of soul-searching into two minutes. 'So what do you think happens to us when we die?'

It was a question I'd asked a lot since the accident, and I was anxious to hear our esteemed head student's considered response. Rob the Slob was about to illuminate one of the great mysteries of the universe when someone I was *definitely* hoping to avoid stuck her head round the door.

'Can I have a quick word, Chris?'

Luke Corcoran morphed from philosopher to philistine in the blink of an eye. 'You can have a word with him if you want, but it don't mean you'll get one back!' Luke Corcoran really *did* cackle.

'Yes, that's very funny,' said Ariel. 'Come on, Chris. It won't take a minute.'

I didn't want the whole school knowing I'd visited her

caravan at half-term, so I followed Ariel into the corridor and stood beneath the *Careless Talk Costs Lives* poster, trying not to give anything away.

'I just wanted to make sure you were OK,' she said. 'Did you enjoy the rest of the holiday?'

I couldn't help thinking that back in 1939 I'd have just been doing my bit for the war effort.

'I meant what I said, you know. As soon as you feel like talking, you've got to promise to come and find me. In fact, why don't you come out to *Honesty* at the weekend? It looks like we're in for a cold snap. Mum and I are going to swaddle the wormeries with bubble wrap.'

Ariel was like a truth drug. The longer I spent with her, the more likely I was to crack. She seemed to have worked out I was hiding something. And she wasn't going to let it go.

'You were doing so well until Will Hunt turned up. There's something you want to tell me, I know there is. Just think how much better you'll feel when you've got it off your chest.'

She couldn't have been more wrong about the last thing. The gaps between the tidal waves of guilt were getting shorter now. I was in urgent need of some pain relief.

'Or I could pop over to yours sometime,' said Ariel. 'In fact, I think I know something that might help us both. You see, what we could —'

'Hey, you two!' called a commanding voice from the end of the corridor. 'Seen any good mutant zombies lately?'

'It's all right,' said Ariel calmly. 'Just ignore him. We can go out to the courtyard if you like.'

Will Hunt's laugh was more like a volley of machine gun fire. 'That was so brilliant. I just wish I'd filmed it all.'

'Look, I'm not being funny or anything,' said Ariel, 'but we're trying to have a private conversation here. Come on, Chris, let's go outside.'

Will eased out of his brown leather gloves. 'And what if he doesn't want to? There is such a thing as free will, you know.'

'All right then,' said Ariel, giving me a quick taste of her guilt inducing irises. 'I'm going outside for a bit. You can come along too if you like, Chris.'

She walked slowly down the corridor. My feet twitched uneasily on the cold concrete. A big part of me wanted to go after her, but I knew that if I followed Ariel, she'd just keep trying to wear me down.

'That was awkward,' said Will, the warmth of his smile practically setting the school on fire. 'Look, I hope you didn't mind me butting in like that. You looked a bit . . . uncomfortable, that's all. Anyway, I'm glad you're here because I'm just a *leetle* bit excited about something.'

Ariel reached the end of the corridor. She turned

back expectantly. A fresh wave of guilt threatened to knock me sideways.

'You remember what I was saying the other night?' said Will. 'Well, I think it's about time you and me started having some of that serious fun I was talking about.' He glanced up at the *Careless Talk Costs Lives* poster. 'I'm not telling you right now because it's probably more exciting to keep you guessing for a bit. Oh, but don't worry,' he said mysteriously, 'everything will be revealed in due course.'

Will Hunt had taken your place in the low-achievers PE group. The sporting elite of St Thomas's were despatched to the four corners of the school field for their inter-house football matches and hockey tournaments, whilst we wound-up the latest supply teacher with our legendary inability to kick, run or throw without even breaking sweat.

'Lovely day for it, sir,' said Will, looking up at the black cloud that was already spitting on us. 'Perfect cross country weather.'

'Can we go in the gym, sir?' said the girl who puked on the war graves trip. 'It's going to pour down in a minute.'

'How about another lecture on health and nutrition?' said Rob the Slob.

The new man in the tracksuit had already perfected his sadistic smile. 'This guy's right,' he said, nodding approvingly at Will. 'The conditions are almost perfect for long distance running.'

Everyone groaned. No self-respecting low achiever would ever contemplate running – unless it was to avoid a tackle or drop a catch. What the hell was Will playing at?

'Don't forget to stretch your hamstrings,' said the man in the tracksuit. 'And then we'll have three laps of the field. It looks like you lot could do with the exercise.'

'Don't worry, I haven't gone completely barking,' whispered Will, as we lined up next to the long-jump pit and waited for Rob the Slob to complete his elaborate stretching routine. 'This is a little trick I picked up at prep school. Stick with me and you'll be fine.'

We were all tortoises in the low achievers group, so it was something of a shock when Will set off like the fabled hare. 'Come on, keep up,' he growled, splattering Rob the Slob's pristine PE vest with thick brown mud and sprinting towards the football pitches.

Now I realised how Rupert felt. I didn't know where the next breath was coming from. Keeping pace with Will was making me so dizzy with exhaustion I could barely make out the dulcet tones of Darren Denyer swearing at his defenders for failing to correctly execute the offside trap.

By the time we came to the Demon Headmaster's 'conservation area' – or Shangri-*bla* as you so wittily called it, Declan – we were so far ahead of the pack that no one saw Will Hunt pull up abruptly and lead me across to the hut where the old groundsman bloke kept his motor mower. 'Right,' said Will, taking his pulse with his index finger. 'We'll hide behind here until the last one goes past. We've got about eight minutes to get into school and back again.'

You're probably wondering why I followed him. It was addictive, the adrenalin rush. What made it all so exciting was that you never really knew what he might come up with next. And while I was stressing over Will's latest escapade, it was much more difficult to live in the past.

'Just relax and enjoy it,' he said, crawling past the all-weather hockey pitches towards the temporary class-rooms. 'I know exactly what I'm doing. Time spent in reconnaissance is seldom time wasted – as my grandfather used to say.'

Loitering outside the changing rooms, it seemed that Will had overlooked an important detail. But as soon as Miss Stanley's 'lost geographers' had disappeared round the corner with their sketch maps, he produced a shiny key from his tennis shorts.

'The security in this place is terrible.' He smiled, slipping into the changing rooms and locking the door behind us. 'Good grief, does no one take a shower in here?'

He'd obviously done his homework. It took him twenty seconds to locate the oversized school jacket he was looking for. 'This may look simple,' he said, reaching into the inside pocket. 'But let me tell you something, Christopher, world wars have started over less.'

Everyone knew that Darren Denyer had the latest generation of smartphone. He'd been flashing his apps at everyone in Year Eleven. I wasn't sure what it was capable of exactly but, knowing him, it could probably smash your face in and then come up with the perfect alibi. And he was probably the only kid at St Thomas's who would have left it in the changing rooms. You'd have had to be some kind of an idiot to mess with Darren Denyer. So what was Will playing at?

'Right,' he said, offering me a quick glimpse of the fastest, sleekest most desirable smartphone in the universe until next week. 'Let's do it, shall we?'

Will took a step sideways to the next peg. Luke Corcoran's rucksack was unmistakable. It was 'pimped to the max' with biro drawings of his favourite parts of the male and female anatomy and some of his more 18-rated philosophical musings.

'Let's not make it too difficult for them,' said Will, carefully positioning Darren Denyer's phone in the front pocket of Luke Corcoran's rucksack, and unzipping it just enough to give the whole world a tantalising glimpse of its high-resolution touchscreen. 'Let's face it, neither of them is terribly bright.'

I couldn't help smiling when I realised what he was up to.

'I'm sure I don't have to spell it out for you, Christopher, but you must *never, ever* tell anyone about this.' Will let out a self-satisfied chuckle. 'Sorry, matey, couldn't resist it.' He opened the door a fraction to scan the courtyard for enemy goons. 'Now let's get the hell out of here. We've got a race to win.'

Most of the low achievers were on their last lap when we got back to the groundsman's hut. The girl who puked on the war graves trip wasn't the only one who was looking peaky. They were all so shattered that no one noticed us tag on behind them and start the slow crawl for home.

It was only when we rounded the final corner and spotted the man in the tracksuit busily texting that Will Hunt broke into a trot. 'This is it,' he said. 'Showtime!'

And he made a pretty good job of simulating exhaustion as we moved quickly through the field and struck out for home.

It was a dead heat. Just for a second, I had an inkling of what it must feel like to be the kind of kid who looks forward to sports day. But Will's performance was the more dramatic, throwing himself over the finishing line and sliding head first towards the man in the tracksuit's trainers.

At first, I thought he was really injured, but he sprang to his feet, looking every inch the courageous winner. 'I think you must have dropped your key, sir.'

His comic timing was so perfect I had to disguise my laughter as a coughing fit.

'Thanks a lot,' said tracksuit man. 'Nice race, by the way. We'll have to see about setting you two some higher targets.'

It sounds pretty mean when I say it now, but I really wanted to see how things would pan out in the changing rooms. And it was almost gratifying to discover that World War Three had already broken out by the time we got there.

'I'll say it again nicely, shall I?' said Darren Denyer, addressing his team mates like the Incredible Hulk on a bad hair day. 'Which one of you low life scum has nicked my phone?'

If anything Will was even better at feigning innocence than exhaustion. 'It's Darren, isn't it?' he said. 'What seems to be the trouble?'

Darren Denyer would never be a proper psycho until he acquired his tattoos. 'You saw my phone, didn't you, Geez?'

'Yeah, course,' said Will. 'I think we all did.'

'Some bozo pinched it from my jacket pocket. And when I find out which one of this lot done it, he's going to wish he'd never been born.'

Will stretched out a comforting arm and patted him on the shoulder. 'I'm sure there are no thieves at St Thomas's, Darren. If you ask me there's probably a perfectly reasonable explanation. Why don't we all help you to look?'

'Yeah . . . cheers,' mumbled Darren.

The whole changing room breathed a collective sigh of relief and started doing the sort of over-the-top 'looking acting' you might have seen in the school play.

There's no excuse for what I did next. I just felt this insane urge for a piece of the action. So when Will flashed me an impish smile, I found myself drifting towards Luke Corcoran's graffiti-laden rucksack. Stamping on the floor for attention, I pointed innocently at the glistening touchscreen in the front pocket.

Will burst out laughing. 'Oh Darren, you're never going to believe this.'

Darren Denyer flexed his knuckles. '*What* did you say?'

'I think I see what you've done,' said Will, helpfully. 'You *thought* you'd left it in your jacket pocket, but it's here, look! It must have been in your rucksack all the time.'

Darren Denyer grabbed the love of his life and turned a rather unflattering shade of red. 'Yeah, but it's not my rucksack, is it? It's . . .'

The flash of lightning that fizzed across the changing

room was Luke Corcoran making his getaway. 'I never done it,' he squealed, trying to pull on his trousers and run at the same time.

Darren Denyer shot out a muscular arm and caught him in a headlock. 'Where do you think *you're* going?'

Luke Corcoran turned a rather unflattering shade of white. 'Please, Dazza, you've got to believe me. I would never . . .'

Darren Denyer drew back his XXL-sized fist.

'No, stop!' The voice of reason came from a rather unexpected source. He was like you, Declan, always wanting to push a joke to the limit. 'Violence never solved anything,' said Will. 'Now I'm not denying it looks bad, but there are bound to be extenuating circumstances. Perhaps Luke's been having a hard time at home.'

'Do me a favour,' said Darren Denyer, smashing Luke's head into the lockers. 'I should have known it was him in the first place.'

Luke Corcoran rolled instinctively into a ball on the changing room floor. Darren Denyer planted a size ten football boot in his stomach.

The cry of 'Fight, fight fight,' went up.

Mr Moore, the head of PE, arrived in the nick of time. 'All right, all right,' he shouted, adding a couple of blasts on his whistle for good measure. 'What's all this noise about?'

Luke Corcoran dragged himself to his feet, sniffing a gobbet of blood back up into his left nostril.

'Oh it's *you*, Corcoran,' said Mr Moore, 'I might have known. Do we have a problem here?'

Luke Corcoran looked up at Darren Denyer and then sideways at Mr Moore. 'No, sir.'

'Good,' said Mr Moore, taking out his fancy new stop-watch. 'Now, *when* I return – in precisely eight minutes and thirty-two point five seconds – I want you lot out of here. *Do* I make myself clear?'

There was a chorus of 'Yes, sirs' and a 'Perfectly' from Will as Mr Moore cowboy-walked back to his office.

'Right,' said Darren Denyer. 'Someone watch the door.'

I've never really liked Luke Corcoran. After some of the stuff he did to me in Year Eight (I actually faked a grumbling appendix to avoid that trip to the cheese factory) it should have been therapeutic to see him taking such a comprehensive beating. But it wasn't. Luke was pretty harmless underneath it all. And although I'd kind of enjoyed the build-up, the punch-line was hard to stomach. Darren Denyer had all the restraint of a cage fighter. When he moved in to finish him off, I had to look away.

And that's when Will Hunt sidled up next to me and whispered, 'He deserves it, anyway. Have you seen what he's like with some of those Year Sevens? And nice work by the way; loved the pointing thing.'

When Darren Denyer's retribution was finally complete, he dragged Luke Corcoran under the shower and threw his rucksack after him. 'And don't you dare get out until you're completely soaked.'

The rest of them fled to the courtyard. Will stayed behind to play the Good Samaritan. 'I'm afraid you're going to have a humdinger of a black eye,' he said, helping Luke to his feet and handing him his soggy rucksack. 'I'm really sorry about that, Luke. I had no idea it was yours. And I'm sure Christopher didn't either.'

'Forget it,' said Luke, balancing on one foot so he could hold his trouser leg up to the new hand dryer. 'I was just in the wrong place at the wrong time.'

Will had a spring in his step the size of a moon-walker's as we crossed the courtyard to our next lesson. 'I bet that took your mind off your problems, didn't it, Christopher?'

When I thought about it, I realised he was right. I'd hardly given you a second thought since registration, Declan. What's more, there's a distinct possibility I would have made it right through to the final bell, if Ariel hadn't ambushed me after English.

'You know what, you're an idiot. Poor Luke was in a terrible state. And don't play the innocent because I know you and your floppy-haired friend had something to do with it. I mean, do you honestly believe Declan would want you hanging out with someone like Will Hunt? Grow up, Christopher. It's not what you need right now. If you carry on like this, something really bad could happen.'

Twelve Weeks
After The Crash

But it didn't stop me hanging out with Will Hunt. Because for a couple of weeks at least it really did take my mind off the bad stuff. I mean, none of it was life threatening or anything (well, not yet anyway) and some of the stunts we pulled were verging on genius. Honestly, Declan, you would have enjoyed it more than anyone. In fact, I sometimes caught myself wishing you could be there.

It was worth the twenty-minute wait in the bushes just to see the look of despair on the Demon Headmaster's face after we egged his precious car. 'Serves him right for driving a crappy BMW,' said Will. And when Rob the Slob fished his page-a-day diary out of the music block toilets, he actually spawned a new school catchphrase: *An accident? I think not.*

One morning in RE, I rediscovered the pleasure of having the whole class laughing *with* me and not at me for a change. Tash Wilson was in the middle of a fully-fledged nervous breakdown having discovered bubble gum in her recently highlighted hair. 'What kind of monster would do a thing like that?' she screeched. 'Well, one of you must have seen who it was?' Like you said, comedy is all about timing, so when she turned to me and demanded, 'What about you, Chris?', I made a gormless face and pointed at my speechless mouth.

But it didn't last. Although Ariel gave up trying to show me the error of my ways, her silent disapproval followed me round the school like a nasty smell. It was her version of Mrs Woolf's 'Not angry, just disappointed' routine – only in Ariel's case it actually made me feel guilty.

Perhaps that's why I started seeing you again, Declan. Well, not seeing you exactly. It was more a case of serial mistaken identity. I'd spot someone in the dinner queue or at the end of the corridor and, just for a millisecond, I could have sworn it was you. Don't get all big-headed about it, but they were the happiest milliseconds I'd had in months. Of course, as soon as I looked again and released I was mistaken, the disappointment was so overwhelming I sometimes had to find an empty classroom to cry in.

I tried telling myself they were understandable mistakes. Plenty of kids at St Thomas's needed a decent haircut, and we all looked the same in school uniform. But then you started cropping up on TV – sipping a strawberry milkshake in Central Perk, loitering behind that girl you fancied in *Skins*, assisting drawmaster Willy at the national lottery. That didn't seem quite so understandable – and hats off to Dr Tennant for interpreting my customary silence as a little more 'difficult' than usual. In fact, it was so frightening that I even fantasised about telling Ariel the whole story. Luckily I didn't try to go through with it.

Will must have sensed something was wrong, because one Saturday morning he turned up at our house wearing his voluminous black trench coat and an even bigger smile. 'I've come to take Chris shopping, Mrs Hughes,' he said. 'I thought his wardrobe could do with a serious update.'

'That's very kind of you, Will,' said Mum. 'And you've brought your own bags I see.'

'If my step-mother is prepared to chain herself to a tree for three days, the least I can do for the environment is a bit of recycling,' said Will.

Mum glanced anxiously across at the sofa to where I was pretending to read Dad's paper. 'Well, you can ask him if you like, but I'm not sure he'll want to go.' She lowered her voice to a stage whisper, so that only me, Will and the bloke painting his garage at number sixty-four could hear. 'I thought he was making progress, and then suddenly it's like we're back to square one again. He's even stopped watching television.'

'I could try talking to him if you like,' said Will. 'I think what he really needs is a friend right now.'

'Yes, yes, you're right,' said Mum, spotting a fleck of dust on the TV screen and pummelling it with her sleeve. 'I'll leave you to it, shall I?'

Will waited for her to retreat to the kitchen before joining me on the sofa. 'How's it going, matey? Your mum says you've been a bit . . .'

I stared at Dad's newspaper, hoping your face wouldn't appear in the gossip column.

'Look, I think I might know what this is all about,' said Will.

I was quite sure that he didn't.

'I was the same, you know. Once you've tasted a bit of excitement, you keep craving more.' He took Dad's newspaper and laid it on the arm of the sofa. 'Well, don't worry. What I've got lined up for this morning is every bit as electrifying as your first black run at Val d'Isère. So come on, Christopher, why don't you get your coat?'

I was so desperate I would probably have tried anything.

Mum was in the hallway brandishing twenty-pound notes. '*You'd* better look after the money, William,' she said. 'Chris can be a bit . . . forgetful at the moment.'

'No need to worry about cash, Mrs Hughes,' said

Will. 'I was planning on using Dad's credit card. I know they're making a few redundancies at head office, but he still got a pretty decent bonus this year. Not that your husband's in any danger, of course,' he added with an amiable smile.

'Well, that's good to know,' said Mum, 'but take it anyway.'

'If you insist,' said Will, slipping the crisp notes into his overcoat. 'Don't worry, I'll see to it that he's home for lunch. I'm sure he'll have a smile on his face by then.'

I was far from smiling when we reached the shopping centre and Will told me what he had in mind.

'Shoplifting is halfway between a sport and an art. To do it properly you need the reflexes of a tennis pro and the acting skills of Robert De Niro.'

You know what I'm like about sticking to the rules, Declan. I get all twitchy if my library books are overdue. And shoplifting is actually illegal; shoplifting is the first step on the rocky road to juvenile delinquency.

'Don't worry,' said Will, leading me over to the empty bench in front of Santa and his elves. 'We'll start you off on the bunny slopes. But before we let you loose on the public, I think I'd better talk you through the basics.'

By the time he'd finished, I was sweating like that French teacher we had in Year Eight – and it wasn't just because Will had insisted I wear my heaviest coat. I was so terrified of being hauled off down to the police station or spending Christmas in a young offenders' institute, that I only caught selected highlights of his master class: *Confidence is paramount . . . Try to find the blind spots . . . Store detectives are rarely deductive geniuses . . . There are at least three different ways to disable a security tab . . .*

So what made me follow him into that trendy new clothes shop opposite Boots? Simple really: even a store detective could have figured it out. It was the busiest Saturday of the year and yet, for all those thousands of people milling about, I hadn't spotted a single Declan Norris lookalike.

'Right,' said Will, greeting the greeter at the front of the store with a friendly nod. 'I'm going to "try some things on". Now you know what to do. Just act suspiciously.'

It wasn't hard. I must have looked as guilty as that bloke in the Shakespeare play, whose wife keeps telling him to murder people, and anyone who knew me even slightly would have realised how out of place I felt in a store that sold paisley neckerchiefs and skinny cord suits.

Will had demonstrated how to examine an item and then make it look like you were going to slip it into your bag before returning it to the shelf at the last moment. And I was obviously pretty good at it because ten minutes later Will emerged from the changing area and gave me the signal to make my way to the front of the store.

I hung the pale crème crop-top back on the rail and

made a beeline for the main entrance. Pure relief turned to undiluted panic when I stepped back into the shopping mall and someone grabbed me by the wrist.

'Could I have a quick word, please, sir?'

He might not have been Sherlock Holmes, but I was still wetting myself.

'What's your name, son?' said the burly security guard in the charcoal chinos.

I knew I couldn't speak; it was a shock to discover that I couldn't move either.

'All right, if that's the way you want to play it. Can I see inside the bags, please?'

Before we left the house, Will had presented me with a couple of half empty designer carriers. I hadn't a clue what was in them.

'Look, we can either do this *my* way, or the hard way. Now can I see in the bags, please, sir?'

Two beads of perspiration were joyriding down my back when Will sauntered out of the shop, his overcoat bulging. 'I think you'd better show him,' he said.

'And who might you be?' said the man in charcoal.

'I'm looking after him for the day,' said Will. 'Is there a problem here?'

'Well, yes, there is actually. This gentleman has refused to give me his name.'

'And do you make a habit of harassing troubled teenagers?' said Will, somehow managing to flash me a reassuring wink at the same time as folding his arms across his protruding stomach.

The security guard let go my wrist. 'All he had to do was tell me his name.'

Will lapsed abruptly into hard-hitting-documentary mode. 'And if you'd shown any sensitivity whatsoever, you would have realised that Christopher here can't talk. Mutism may not be as glamorous as some of the other disabilities, but I've seen what it does to families.'

The security guard took a long hard look at me. 'So why was he hanging around in ladies' fashions?'

'We've been out Christmas shopping for his mother. She's had a rough ride of it herself lately – isn't that right, Christopher?'

Will's enthusiasm was so infectious that it was practically impossible not to crack a smile, but I nodded slowly and tried to look as pathetic as one of those kids in *The County Times* who's had his bike nicked.

'I think you'd better show him what's in the bag,' said Will. 'The poor man's only doing his job.'

Like I said, I didn't know what was in them, but I had a funny feeling Will would be every bit as prepared as the keenest boy scout when it came to shoplifting. So I reached into the first carrier, rummaged around a bit like a bad magician, and pulled out . . . some sleeping pills from the health food shop, a self-confidence CD by that hypnotherapist bloke, a book about coping with divorce, a cuddly puppy thing with a yellow nose . . .

The security guard had seen enough. 'Yeah, all right,' he said. 'Maybe I got it wrong. It's not easy sometimes.'

'No problemo,' said Will, generously. 'You weren't to know. Here, take this.' He placed a twenty-pound note in the security guard's top pocket. 'Call it an early Christmas present. I feel sorry for you.'

And before he could protest, Will had guided me past the Sky TV man and onto the escalator. 'I bet you're buzzing, aren't you, matey?' he said, pulling out a silk scarf and twisting it playfully round my neck. 'Now, where shall we try next?'

We continued in the same vein until Will's carrier bags were swollen with booty. To 'stop it getting samey', he'd compiled a list of random items for us to shoplift, like a scavenger hunt. He was right, I really was buzzing. But you know the best thing of all? It almost felt like being in a double act again – only this time *I* was the funny one. Looking gawky and nervous came naturally, and I was almost starting to enjoy myself when we walked away from Mothercare and Will broke it to me.

'Right, the last one on my list is a shoplifter's staple, the humble CD. Doesn't have to be anything in particular, just go for the first one that takes your fancy.'

I felt my face contort into a Halloween mask of horror.

'Yes, that's right,' said Will, checking out the manager's special in the window. 'This time it's your turn, my friend. Come on, Christopher, it'll do you the power of good. Believe me, you'll feel so much better once you've tried it.'

The well-known high street music outlet was thumping in time with my heart. You know the store I'm talking about, Declan. You once tried to convince me that the initials stood for something disgusting. Will went straight to the Xbox games and started doing a bizarre decoy dance while I had a crisis of conscience in Easy Listening.

Being an accomplice was one thing, but doing the deed myself was a completely different kettle of fish. Mum would kill me if she found out. Hadn't she had enough to deal with lately? I knew it was wrong, but I half remembered something Mr Catchpole said in PSHE about how sometimes doing a bad thing can be the lesser of two evils. Maybe Will was right; maybe it really would make me feel better. So I checked the heavens for CCTV cameras and reached for a rather tragic-looking CD.

According to Will, the security tag was supposed to come off easily; now that I was biting my nails again I just couldn't get the stupid thing to budge. But what the hell? Taking risks was the whole point, wasn't it? So I slipped it into my pocket anyway. The funny thing is I'd never felt more alive. Nothing else mattered. I could see everything in such ultra high-definition that it was almost like having superpowers. No one on earth could stop me now.

As soon as the alarm went, I started running; forcing my way through the hordes of hyped-up shoppers, avoiding the life-sized sculpture of the roller-skating pensioners, and another Sky TV man, before charging down the escalator with Santa's blessing ringing in my ears. 'Don't forget late night shopping on Thursday. There's free parking after seven o' clock. Ho! Ho! Ho!'

My superpowers told me I was still being followed, but I didn't even bother to look back. There was so much adrenalin coursing through my veins that I knew I'd be able to accelerate through the underpass like a sports day kid. And I was halfway round the park before my breathing started getting so heavy that I decided to take a quick peek.

'All right, sonny . . . you're *nicked*,' panted Will with a huge smile.

You should have heard us laugh.

Back at the house, we handed out presents, like a dodgy Santa and his non-speaking elf: a pack of disposable toilet seat covers for Pete ('Awesome'), a garden gnome with a tennis racket for his friend Gary Lulham ('Thanks, dude') and a cardigan for Mum, which she said was 'lovely' but was sure to try and take back even without the receipt.

'Why don't you boys go upstairs and I'll bring you some bacon sarnies?' she said.

'Thanks, Mrs Hughes,' said Will, checking out his new shades in the hall mirror. 'That's really kind of you.'

'No, thank *you*, Will,' said Mum. 'I don't know how you managed it, but it's so nice to see him smiling again.'

And for a while, the adrenalin kept working its magic. After we'd wolfed down our bacon sandwiches and an assortment of random confectionary, Will slapped on the *Very Best of Mantovani and his Orchestra* and I waltzed round the bedroom in my new ensemble. I couldn't quite see how a khaki T-shirt and a skinny cord blazer, some black vintage jeans, a pork pie hat and a belted, camel trench coat could go together, but Will said I looked like some actor I'd never heard of.

'It's funny how things work out, isn't it?' he said, lying down on my bed and playing with the plastic pineapple cutter we'd nicked from the pound shop. 'You needed a friend, and I was in the right place at the right time. It almost feels like fate or something.'

The adrenalin was wearing off. If there is such a thing as fate, then maybe all the bad stuff that happened is part of some preordained plan – and maybe there was worse to come.

'Don't worry,' said Will. 'I've got plenty of ideas. We could do something tomorrow if you like.'

I'd kept you out of my head for nearly four hours, Dec, but I couldn't help remembering that first meeting of ours in the nursery sandpit; now *that* felt like destiny.

'Knock, knock,' sang Mum, pushing open the door without waiting for a response. 'Visitor for you, Chris. How about that, two friends in one day? At least, she tells me she's a friend,' said Mum, going off on a badly conceived comic riff. 'I mean she'd hardly say she was your friend if she wasn't, would she? That would be like, well . . . I don't know what like . . .'

Ariel was standing in the doorway, a canvas sports bag slung over one shoulder. The mere sight of her was sometimes enough to send me hurtling back to the night of Ella's party, but I couldn't help feeling strangely relieved that she hadn't given up on me.

Will's face seemed to cloud over when he saw who it was. 'Ariel's in our English group, Mrs Hughes. What she doesn't know about witches in *The Crucible* isn't worth knowing.'

'That's nice, dear,' said Mum, smiling doubtfully at Ariel. 'And you say you've brought something to cheer Chris up?'

'Well, I hope so anyway,' said Ariel. 'I just want to do something to help.'

'I'll leave you guys to it, then,' said Mum, looking pathetically pleased at my newfound popularity. 'Give me a shout if you need a drink.'

130

The door clicked shut. I'd experienced a lot of awkward silences since my voice packed up, but this one was right up there with the very worst. If I'd still been able to speak, I would have told them your gag about the talking greyhound as an icebreaker.

'Hi, Chris,' mumbled Ariel, shuffling her still-slightly-muddy feet on the pale blue carpet. 'How are you doing?'

I sank onto my Pokémon beanbag, struggling to maintain any dignity in a pork pie hat.

'He's doing fine,' said Will. 'At least he was until a minute ago.'

Ariel tried to catch my eye; I sank a little further into the beanbag.

'And what's all this about cheering him up?' said Will. 'Does he look unhappy?'

'Well, yes, he does actually,' said Ariel. 'That's why I'm here.'

Will gnawed the end of the plastic pineapple cutter. 'OK, so what exactly have you got in mind?'

Ariel shuffled a little more dried mud onto the carpet. 'I just wanted to —'

'And what's in the bag?' said Will. 'Come on, Ariel, show and tell!'

'It's . . . private,' she said, blushing slightly and tightening her grip on the sports bag.

'Oh, come on,' said Will. 'I won't tell anyone, promise.'

Ariel paused for a moment, chewing thoughtfully on

her bottom lip. 'I think I'd better leave it for now. Sorry, Chris, I should have you realised you might be busy. Don't worry, I'll come back tomorrow.'

Spending time with Ariel was like being permanently wired to a lie detector, so why did I feel a hint of disappointment as she slipped out of the door?

'I'd better get off too,' said Will, stashing some half-eaten family packs of Haribos into his carrier bag. 'Holly's picking me up in Sainsbury's car park. But we should definitely do this again sometime. Catch you later.'

And I thought he'd gone, until I realised he was still hovering in the doorway. 'She'll only want to talk at you, you know. I mean, maybe you can cope with that, but I'm guessing it's the last thing you need right now.'

He was probably right. The trouble is, no matter how hard I tried to ignore it, one question had pummelled its way into the forefront of my mind: What on earth was in Ariel's bag?

I didn't have to wait long to find out. At about three o' clock on Sunday afternoon, Mum stood outside my bedroom and sang 'Knock, knock'. I couldn't understand why she always made a sound effect when the real thing was right there in front of her, or why she bothered in the first place, considering she'd never waited to be invited in, even when I could talk.

'Friend to see you,' she said. 'Come on, Ariel, don't be shy.'

'Thanks very much, Mrs Hughes,' said Ariel, the same canvas sports bag still hanging from her shoulder. 'This won't take long.'

'Oh right,' said Mum, withdrawing as tactfully as she knew how. 'Don't forget to give me a call if you need anything.'

What did Ariel want exactly? And why did I always feel guilty when she smiled at me like that?

'It's something I thought we could do together,' she said, dumping her sports bag on my bed and then starting to unzip it. 'It might sound a bit lame, but I think it could actually help.'

She took out a small wicker basket. On the lid was a piece of cloth embroidered with the words *Declan Norris – Memory Box*.

It felt like someone had just tap-danced across my grave.

'Inside are some of the things that remind me most of Declan. Perhaps after we've had a look, you could add some of your own.' She sat down on my bed and unfastened the catch. 'It's supposed to help you move on.'

It sounded like the very worst kind of psychobabble. Even so, I couldn't help wondering what Ariel had chosen, so I sat down beside her, and she opened the box.

'Some Native Americans believe that if you take their photograph, you capture their soul. I reckon this one captures Declan's pretty perfectly, don't you?'

She handed me a slightly crumpled photo with the remains of four blobs of Blu-tack on the back. It was your life all right, but not as we knew it. I'd certainly never seen you with a spade in your hand, and the serious face you were pulling kind of gave me the same feeling I got when Mum used words like 'wicked'.

'My dad took it,' said Ariel. 'I don't see him that much.'

Like I said, it was a dumb idea, but she'd obviously made an effort so I thought I ought to play along. And besides, I didn't think the only photograph in your memory box should look like a moody philosopher digging an allotment.

I'd ripped it down the day after the accident, but the picture I took in Ypres was still at the back of the wardrobe where I'd hidden it. I handed it to Ariel.

'That is *so* nice,' she said. 'You took that on the war graves trip, didn't you?'

I nodded.

'You have no idea how much I wanted to talk to him. I tried all sorts of things: making awful jokes, pretending I knew something about First World War poetry – I even changed my hair.'

That didn't sound like Ariel at all.

'I thought he wasn't interested, but I must have dropped so many hints that one day he turned up at the caravan and asked if I wanted to see that Al Gore movie about climate change. Mum gave him three pots of apple chutney in exchange for the tickets. And he didn't even tease me about it!'

And *that* didn't sound like *you*, Declan.

'It was only on in Brighton, so we took the train.' She pulled out a ticket for the Duke of York's cinema and another for Network South East. 'Afterwards we walked down to the end of the pier. That was the best part really.'

No wonder you were so secretive about your trip to Brighton. I scrabbled round under the bed for a DVD to redress the balance. Parallel universe Declan might have been happy watching the ice-caps melt, but I never heard you laugh louder than the first time we saw *Wayne's World 2*.

'He loved this movie, didn't he?' said Ariel. 'Did he ever show you his impression of the roadie guy?'

Only about three-hundred-and-sixty-five-million times.

'I'll put it in the box, shall I?'

I wanted to tell her about your controversial view that *WW2* was better than the original (and you're still wrong, by the way), but I just nodded and smiled.

'I'm not sure what to say about this last one,' she said, her cheeks flushing slightly as she handed me a sheet of

A4. 'No one had ever written me a song before.' Her eyes were clouding over. 'Declan was full of surprises.'

You can say that again. If I hadn't recognised your crappy left-handed writing and all the crossings out, I would have sworn it was a fake.

If I wrote a song that made you out to be a paragon
Would you laugh at me?
If I said that you're all right, with bourgeoisie clichés
through the night
Would you ~~stay to tea~~ run away?

Ariel snatched it back from me. 'Do you mind reading it some other time? I'm just a bit . . .'

I handed her the packet of baby wipes that Will had taken from Mothercare.

'Thanks,' she said, dabbing her cheeks. 'Now, what about you? Is there anything else you'd like to put in?'

It was the most precious thing in my possession. Everyone knew how careless you were. It was totally your fault that I'd deleted it from my hard drive in the first place, so it made perfect sense that I was the one who guarded it with my life.

'This looks interesting,' said Ariel, as I felt for the key on top of the wardrobe.

The only existing copy of the first episode of our sitcom *The Capped Crusader* was safely stashed in a metal cash box under my bedside table. In the event of fire, it was the first thing I would have rescued after Mum and Dad – and possibly Pete.

I turned the key in the lock. Even though I checked on it nearly every day, it was still a relief to see it lying there.

'Oh my God,' said Ariel. 'It's your sitcom about the traffic warden with superpowers. You have no idea how proud he was of this.'

I placed eighteen-and-a-half pages of badly typed television script into her trembling hands.

'Great title by the way. Dec said it was one of yours.' She started flicking through it, pointing out some of the gags. '*Just the ticket, sir* . . . that's really funny.'

It was probably our favourite fantasy of all time: a pretty girl laughing at our jokes. And for a while at least, I forgot the bad stuff and just focused on all the good times. It didn't even matter that Ariel's version of you seemed such a contrast to mine. It reminded me of that quantum physics thing that Rob the Slob was always going on about where two scientists could come to completely different conclusions about the same object and yet both be right. So I was actually a little bit disappointed when she replaced the lid and got up to leave.

'I'd better go. You've seen what my mum's like about meditation.' She rolled her eyes and made a funny face. 'It won't bring him back or anything, but maybe it's good for both of us to remember him now and then.'

I handed her the precious box.

'No, keep it,' she said. 'I made it for you.'

I hadn't used Mum's speech cards since someone slipped in a rogue batch containing such useful phrases as *Smell my butt, Mr Catchpole, Permission to burn the school down, Miss* and *I am a chronic sufferer from verbal constipation*, but I selected an old one from the pile on the bookcase and flashed it at her. *Thank you, Miss.*

I've never been lucky enough to hear a nightingale sing, but I'm guessing that Ariel's laughter has the same legendary, uninhibited quality. 'You're welcome,' she said, hesitating for a moment when she reached the door. 'Look, I'm sorry to keep going on about it, but I just know you want to tell me something, Chris. We've got that theatre trip next week. Maybe we could sit together on the coach. That lot are like a bunch of zombies once they get their earphones in. Anyway, think about it.'

And I *did* think about it. In fact, it was *all* I could think about for the next few days. Like the advert, Ariel's memory box did exactly what it said on the tin. Remembering the happy times with her had seemed like a pretty good idea. But after she'd gone, it took about two minutes for the warm glow of nostalgia to flare into a raging forest fire of regret.

Collapsing on my bed in a maelstrom of snotty sobbing, I wrapped my arms around the small wicker basket, half believing that if I could keep a lid on my memories, my secret would still be safe.

I don't know how long I'd been crying. It might have been five minutes later, or it could easily have been an hour, when I heard loud banging on the front door followed by the sound of galloping feet on the stairs. Mum hadn't even had the chance to sing 'Knock knock' before Will burst into my bedroom.

'All right, matey, how's it —? Hey, what's up? Not down in the dumps again, are we? I thought you'd still be buzzing after yesterday.'

My saturated pillow could no longer contain my sobbing.

'Don't tell me – Ariel, right? I passed her on the way here. What's that ridiculous girl been saying to you now?'

I felt him standing over me, like a paramedic at a motorway pile-up.

'And what's this? *Declan Norris – Memory* . . .? Oh no. She hasn't, has she?' He sat on the edge of my bed, his aftershave drowning the lingering aroma of bacon. 'Don't mind if I have a look inside, do you?'

I *did* mind. But I was weak from all that crying and there was something about his bedside manner that made me loosen my hold.

Will took one look in the box before swiftly replacing the lid. 'Well, no wonder you're upset.'

Upset didn't really cover it.

'Memories are all very well,' said Will, 'but, like I said, sometimes it's better to try and forget – and I ought to know, believe me.' His aftershave retreated as he stood up and started pacing. 'Look, I'm not quite sure how to say this. I mean, he looks like such a fun guy. But the thing is . . . Declan's dead, Christopher. Don't you think it's time to move on?'

And suddenly I knew exactly what to do. An hour ago they'd seemed like precious memories; now I could see how they were dragging me downwards into a spiral of despair. Grabbing hold of the wicker basket, I stumbled across my bedroom and kicked open the door.

'No, wait,' said Will, grabbing his fedora and racing after me as I hurtled downstairs. 'I've got an idea. Why don't I take you —?'

Mum was doing the ironing in front of the telly. 'Is everything all right, Will? I thought I heard banging.'

'Everything's fine,' he said. 'Christopher's been showing me his . . . CD collection.'

Dad was sprawled across the sofa beneath the Sunday papers. He woke with a start when he heard me rattling the French windows. 'You won't tell Dominic I've been slacking, I hope,' he joked.

'Don't worry, Mr Hughes,' said Will, glancing anxiously at my increasingly frenzied attempts to force my way onto the patio.

'Here, let me do that,' said Dad, springing to my aid. 'Honestly, Christopher, you're like a cow with a —'

But I was already halfway to the compost heap, with Will only a couple of steps behind.

'What are you doing, anyway?' he said, following me across the so-called rockery and down past the shed.

All became clear when we arrived at the battered dustbin Dad used for his universally unpopular bonfires. What's that saying? *Out of sight, out of mind.* It sounds crazy now, Declan, but that's exactly what I was thinking when I opened your memory box and poured out the contents.

'Hang on a minute,' said Will, as I turned back towards the house. 'You know what might make you feel even better.' He took out an old-fashioned cigarette lighter and pressed it into my hand. 'I nicked it from my grandfather when he was in hospital. I was doing him a favour really. What do you think gave him terminal cancer in the first place?'

I'm sorry, Declan, but right at that moment, it made perfect sense: *Destroy the memories before the memories destroy you.* I reached into the dustbin and pulled out our sitcom script. It took three clicks before Will's grand-dad's lighter flared into life.

'Why don't you keep it?' said Will. 'It only reminds me of him anyway.'

As soon as it was well and truly blazing, I tossed what

was left of *The Capped Crusader* into the dustbin, and it wasn't long before the crackling inferno was warming my tear-stained cheeks. So it was official then: I might just about have managed to hold it together for the last few months, but as our doomed sitcom sent smoke signals to the great Head of Comedy in the sky, even the dumbest store detective in the universe could see that I'd totally lost it.

'There's no need to cry, matey,' said Will, fanning the flames with his fedora. 'You're doing the right thing, I promise. And hey, we've got that theatre trip to look forward to next week. I know *just* how to cheer you up.'

Thirteen Weeks
After The Crash

Psychiatrist: What seems to be the trouble?
Patient: I can't make any friends.
*   Can you help me, you fat, ugly slob?*

My final session at the CAMHS office started predictably enough. Dr Tennant was running late, as usual, so I sat in the waiting room, vainly scanning the noticeboard for an appropriate helpline. Come to think of it, a helpline for mutes was a pretty dumb idea, but by this time I was beyond desperate and I would have made a pact with the devil, or even taken up country dancing, if I thought it could make things better.

Will's granddad's lighter was still burning a hole in my pocket (no, not literally, Declan; I'm not that stupid). My little bonfire of Hughes and Norris memorabilia was supposed to help me forget. The next morning when I slipped down the garden to rake over the ashes, they only served to remind me of your funeral, and the terrible thing that I'd done.

In fact, I was starting to worry that I might never speak again. It hadn't seemed like such a big deal before, but if I was silenced forever, how would I ever get a job, tell someone I loved them or make prank calls to that gun shop in East Grinstead about getting hold of weapons of mass destruction? More to the point: How would I ever be able to tell anyone how sorry I was? How could I ever tell *you* how sorry I was? If there had been an award for the worst best friend in the universe, I'd have already started work on my acceptance mime.

'All right, Chris?' said Dr Tennant, ushering out the girl in the *Life Sucks* T-shirt. 'Sorry to keep you waiting. I'll be with you in a sec.'

You couldn't fault Dr Tennant for her persistence. I hadn't said a word for practically three months, but she still started with the same old questions and acted like she expected me to respond with a chat-show-guest type anecdote.

'So, how are you feeling?'

Terrible.

'OK then, tell me about school; what sort of week have you had?'

How does an afternoon of shoplifting and a spot of pyromania sound?

'It's fine, you don't have to talk if you don't want to, Chris; let's try something else, shall we? I don't know if we've done this before, but we'll have another go anyway.' She held up a cartoon drawing of an oak tree with a load of stick men and women in the branches. 'Each of the characters represents a different emotion. Which one would you say corresponds most closely to the way you're feeling right now?'

I stared at her exhausted yucca plant, just as I'd done the last six times she'd asked me. The answer in my head had always been the same. It was the guy pushing his friend out of the tree.

'Never mind, we'll try something else,' said Dr Tennant, twirling her pencil like a frustrated cheerleader. 'Now I know you're not wild about role-play, so I think perhaps I should try and explain something about the grieving process again. You see, although different people react to bereavement in different ways, we often find that . . .'

Her voice washed over me like a mountain stream. I tensed every muscle in my body, knowing that if I relaxed for an instant, bad memories were sure to follow. I usually managed to ward them off by making lists. You know the sort of thing, Dec, we did it all the time: our top ten stand-ups, the twenty funniest one-liners, the worst sitcoms in history. But as soon as Dr Tennant began outlining the five stages of grieving, I realised that no list on earth could stop me now. By the time she'd talked through denial and anger, I was already reliving the two minutes that changed our lives forever.

It was the day of Ella's party. Your parents were driving up to Norwich for your sister's graduation thing, so we had the house to ourselves. That's why no one stopped us taking pizza and gummy bears up to your bedroom and why we could spend all afternoon checking out websites of people falling off stuff, with no fear of your dad nagging us to go outside for a bit of exercise. It was raining anyway. Summer was over. Jumpers and hoodies were being resurrected from bottom drawers. And it smelt different too, like burning leaves or something.

As usual, you'd taken control of the laptop. So in a way, it was your fault that I started rooting around in the toxic layer of junk which covered your bedroom carpet. And that, after posing a couple of questions to the Magic 8 Ball (*Is Declan an idiot? All signs point to yes*), I should have reached into the abyss and pulled out a tomato-stained paperback.

'What's this then, Declan?'

'Nothing, give it here.'

I must have sensed your embarrassment. 'Hang on a

minute. *The Self Sufficiency Bible*? Don't tell me you're becoming a tree hugger.'

'I might be,' you muttered. 'Now give it here.'

'Gonna make me?' I said, jumping onto your unmade bed and dancing triumphantly, the book held hostage above my head.

Banter was what we lived for. Exchanging a few humorous insults had to be better than watching some random bloke fall off the back of a pickup truck. So why did you look so angry?

'Look, it's mine, OK? Stop messing about with other people's property.'

My elaborate triple-take was pure poetry. 'Sorry, did Rob the Slob just walk in?'

'I mean it, Chris.'

But I was really getting in to my stride. 'I know, let's have a Bible reading, shall we?' I launched into my best impression of that vicar guy who came into assembly once a year to talk about the 'true meaning of Christmas'. 'The reading this afternoon is taken from *The Self Sufficiency Bible*; beginning to read at page one.'

'Why are you doing this? I thought you were —'

And that's when I saw it; the small, but perfectly formed signature in the top right hand of the inside cover. Why hadn't I realised earlier? I doubted *The Self Sufficiency Bible* had many more jokes than a funeral service, or even an impressive body count. It was hardly typical Declan Norris reading material. 'Wait a minute. I know where this came from.'

Swift as a sparrowhawk, you ripped my legs from under me, snatching back the book as I collapsed head first into your pillow.

'Come on, Chris. Just leave it, OK?'

Part of me wanted to. School etiquette decreed that I carry on lairing you off. 'You got it from that weird girl in our English group; the one who told us to cut off all our designer labels.'

'Her name's Ariel.'

'Yes, I know that,' I said, with a smart-arsed grin. 'She's written her name in the front of your book. Fancy her, do you?'

'Oh yeah, really mature.'

'That's amazing, Declan. Now you even sound like her.'

I waited for the comeback that never came. 'And do you *lurve* each other?'

'Ha, ha.'

'You'd better be careful, Declan. The Beatles were never the same after John Lennon met Yoko whatshername. We don't want the same thing to happen to Hughes and Norris.'

I wasn't sure if you'd understood the Beatles reference, but the glint in your eye looked more like the Declan Norris of old.

'What did you say?'

'I said we don't want the same thing to happen to Hughes and Norris.'

The glint was fast becoming a victorious gleam. 'That's what I thought you said. But you've got it the wrong way round, haven't you . . . *mate*.'

'What are you talking about?' I said, sort of relieved that you weren't taking it lying down.

The gleam was now a rather cruel-looking smile. 'Don't take *my* word for it. Ask anyone at school if you like. Everyone knows it should be Norris and Hughes.'

'It's in alphabetical order,' I said. 'That's the way it's always been.'

'Yeah, but it's wrong, isn't it?' you said, coldly. 'I mean, it makes it look like *you're* top of the bill, Chris. And that can't be right.'

'What . . . Why not?'

You seemed to hesitate. I still wasn't sure if you were messing about. A moment later your words were hurtling towards me like a nuclear warhead.

'BECAUSE YOU'RE NOT FUNNY, MATE.'

OK, so you definitely weren't messing about. My only hope was that I'd misunderstood. 'What did you —?'

'I said, YOU'RE NOT FUNNY.'

All those put-downs we worked on and the only thing I could come up with was a stunned, 'Yes I am.'

'No, you're not, mate. And you've just proved it, with all that pathetic Ariel stuff.'

'I'm just as funny as you are.' (The last time we'd argued was when you accused me of hiding your Lego Hermione.) 'And don't keep calling mate.'

If you'd have stopped right there it's possible we could have patched things up. But you didn't, did you, Declan? That was what made you such a great comedian; sometimes you went just that little bit too far. 'Go on then, prove it,' you said, waving me forward on to an imaginary stage. 'Come on, Mr Funny Man, say something funny.'

All my life I've bottled things up; why did I have to lose it so spectacularly when it really mattered? But what did you expect? You knew full well it was worst thing you could possibly have said.

'So full of yourself, aren't you, Declan? Well, you know what? I don't give a monkey's what you think anyway. So you can stuff your pizza and you can stuff your stupid double-act. I hope I never see your smug-ugly face ever again.'

And that's exactly the way things worked out. Because although you followed me downstairs and called after me as I ran red-faced into the pouring rain, I refused to look back.

'. . . so you see, Chris, "acceptance" can come at any moment, sometimes when you're least expecting it.'

Dr Tennant wound up every session by bludgeoning me over the head with a 'feel good ending' and then reaching into her drawer for a blank sheet of paper. Thank God it was nearly over. Two more minutes and I was sure to crack.

'You remember our first meeting, Chris?' she said, taking a pencil from her *I'D RATHER BE 39* mug and placing it in front of me. 'I asked you to tell me about your friend, the boy who died. And you reacted rather . . . strongly. I don't suppose you feel like talking right now, but perhaps you could write it down instead. So here's a question for you. Why is it that you don't want to talk about Declan?'

Make that two seconds.

Reliving our last moments together had only confirmed what I already knew. But was this "acceptance" or blind stupidity? I took up the pencil in my trembling hand, resting the blunt nib on the pure white paper. The first word came easily.

Because

Writers' block set in almost immediately.

Dr Tennant was starting to look like the child psychiatrist who got the cream. 'Well done, well done, you're doing brilliantly. Just keep going, Chris. This is a real breakthrough.'

Her kind, but overworked and slightly bloodshot, eyes were willing me on. I knew full well that her words of encouragement would count for nothing if she found out the truth.

'That's it, Chris. Just take your time.'

It always looked like such fun in the movies. But my only emotion was acute desperation, as with a yelp of anguish, I swept half her desktop (the comatose yucca, the bulging files of case-notes, the glove puppet who introduced Dr Tennant to timid pre-schoolers) onto the grey carpet tiles.

'Chris, wait, where are you —?'

I never saw her again. Because although she followed me into the corridor and called after me as I ran through a waiting room of troubled adolescents, I refused to look back.

And I kept on running. Not like a sports day kid, but like a fugitive with a guilty secret to protect. If I half-killed myself, I could just about make it there and back before Mum got home from work. Like I said, Declan, I wasn't thinking straight. In fact, that's putting it mildly.

The first part was easy. The wildlife trail had closed already, so it was a relatively simple procedure to slip through a gap in the fence and make my way undetected towards the beetle loggery, guided only by my accomplice, the moon.

The wetlands was full of noises. Out on the lake, the ducks seemed to honk accusingly, a cloud of bats squeaked and swirled overhead, and every time I stepped on a twig or a small creature scuttled for safety, I almost crapped myself. What if someone was spying on me? Will Hunt was probably giving Rupert swimming lessons or peppering tourists with his Kalashnikov, but I couldn't help it. If my mission was to be successful, it was vital there were no witnesses.

The next part was harder; ploughing through the undergrowth in semi-darkness, my face an abstract masterpiece of scratches by the time I emerged. *Honesty Smallholdings* was bathed in moonlight, and the distant caravan glowed uninvitingly. Penny and Ariel were probably still meditating. *Dead to the world*, that's how Penny had described it. In a few more minutes, I'd know if she was right. Reaching into my jacket pocket for the icy lump of metal that was Will's granddad's lighter, I headed reluctantly towards the caravan, trying to tell myself that once it was over, I could rest in peace.

There was chicken poo everywhere, which was fine until I decided to take the last fifty metres on my hands and knees. The whale songs, seeping out from behind the closed curtains, were probably supposed to be relaxing. I couldn't see it myself. Swimming with dolphins never made *my* bucket list (neither did diving for rabbits come to that) and the mere sound of the ocean was enough to make me seasick. No wonder I was a nauseous, nervous wreck by the time I crouched down behind the back window and pondered my next move.

How did I ever come to sink so low? It was my craziest idea yet and, looking back, without any shadow of doubt, my most dangerous. But I was beyond desperate. I'd been within three words of revealing the truth to Dr Tennant. If my actions only stopped those terrible dreams for a couple of nights, it had to be worth a shot.

I pulled out the cigarette lighter and took a few practice clicks.

Like I said, I truly loathed that sculpture. And in some kind of screwed-up way I'd started seeing it as your 'representative on earth'. Faceless and featureless though your effigy was, it felt like you were watching me twenty-four/seven, stalking my nightmares, pointing your angry straw finger and whispering, 'Guilty . . . guilty . . . guilty'. See what I mean, Declan? I told you it was dumb.

I held the flame to the soles of your feet. They flickered for a moment until the wind extinguished them. Next time I managed to shelter you from the elements, and it wasn't long before both your legs were blazing. Forced backwards by the sudden blast of heat, I found myself a hiding place in the trees and watched you burn.

Perhaps meditation wasn't all it was cracked up to be.

Penny didn't look remotely chilled as she threw open the door and invoked the deity. (Screamed 'Oh my God'. Keep up, Declan.) Ariel was hot on her tail. They sprinted across to the water butts, filling bucket after bucket and chucking them at you until the fire was quenched. Luckily for me, they were too late to save you. All that remained were a few strands of chicken wire and a steaming pile of ashes.

Penny put her arm round Ariel and led her back inside. I felt bad about that, but at least neither of them carried mobiles so I wouldn't have to worry about the police turning up. And if I was really lucky, I'd be able to get cleaned up before Mum started asking awkward questions.

Hard though it is to believe now, for a few hours at least, I genuinely believed that it would make things better. You see, the way I looked at it, Declan, I'd just silenced the only other person in the world who knew what I'd done.

Fourteen Weeks
After The Crash

The wind buffeted the luxury coach in the school car park. My mental state was now so fragile that I left it to the last possible moment before vacating my sanctuary in the main reception toilets and stumbling out through the rain.

I should have realised that trying to torch my problems was totally insane. The nightmares were getting darker. Will Hunt's crude attempts at diversion therapy had long since failed to hit the spot, and my waking hours were blighted by bleak visions from the night of the crash. Will said he had 'something special' planned for the *Crucible* trip, but I wasn't holding my breath. Let's face it, apart from that American president guy who got shot, when was the last time anything exciting happened in a theatre?

Rob the Slob was sitting at the front, communing

with his English notes. He'd replaced his vandalised page-a-day diary with an ereader. The haste with which he appeared to have moved on was almost indecent. 'Nice of you to join us,' he said. 'Let's hope there's no flash flooding on the A272.'

'I still don't see why we can't go shopping,' said Tash Wilson, shaking her umbrella over the driver. 'Just because the Big Bad Woolf gets her shoes from an old ladies' catalogue, doesn't mean the rest of us have to.'

The coach was practically full. I hurried past the empty seat beside the girl who puked on the war graves trip and carried on down the aisle, my eyes fixed firmly on the floor.

A hand-knitted glove stopped me in my tracks. 'Come and sit down,' said Ariel. 'I've saved you a place.'

I must have showered at least thirty times since the fire, but the stench of smoke seemed to follow me everywhere. I had to get away from her before she sniffed me out.

'No wait,' she said, fixing me with her truth drug eyes. 'I want to ask you something.'

The rain was hurling itself suicidally against the coach window. If I looked her in the face, I'd be done for.

'It's not just about the crash, is it?' said Ariel. 'There's something else, I know there is; something you can't talk about.'

I turned back to the window, trying to conceal my

shame. Mr Catchpole was running across the car park with a plastic bag on his head.

'You're not sitting with *him*, are you?' said Ariel, as I struggled to push past her. 'You know he set fire to Declan's sculpture, don't you? *I* wanted to call the police, but Mum said it was just a cry for help. Chris, wait! You need to . . .'

Will Hunt was bundling his black trench coat into the overhead luggage rack. 'What's up with her? Not giving you the third degree again, I hope.'

I slipped into the window seat.

'And what's happened to your face? Been out in the dark, have we?'

What if Will *had* been following me? What if he knew about the fire?

'Oh well, never mind,' he said, depositing his phone on the fold-down table attached to the seat in front. 'We'll have some fun when we get there, promise. Which reminds me, Christopher, you really should have brought a coat.'

A muted cheer went up when Mrs Woolf finished her headcount and Mr Catchpole dashed up the steps. 'Sorry about that, Wendy, trouble in the dinner queue.' It was only a matter of time before he started declaiming his 'good citizens' speech. 'Now, I'm sure I don't need to remind anyone that whilst you are in school uniform, you are all —'

If there was any audience participation in *The Crucible*, the actors were sure of a lively response. Virtually the whole coach shouted it back at him, 'AMBASSADORS OF THE SCHOOL!'

'Good,' said Mr Catchpole, nodding at the driver and following Mrs Woolf down the aisle, 'because I haven't forgotten my last school trip.'

'Are you still helping the police with their enquiries, sir?' quipped a would-be comedienne.

Mr Catchpole bared his receding gums. 'Yes, thank you, Becky. I'll do the funnies.'

The coach lurched out of the car park and accelerated into the driving rain. Earphones were inserted and, as the banter faded, you could just make out the distant jangle of hip-hop competing with emo misery and the latest downloads.

Will fired-up his phone and commenced catapulting angry birds at a row of igloos. 'I know Brighton pretty well, actually. Did I tell you my dad's got a place on the marina?'

I waited for him to elaborate. But he was so absorbed in the plight of his belligerent wildfowl that, apart from the occasional expletive, he barely spoke for the rest of the journey, leaving me to sink further into a stupor of despair.

But before I get to the really bad stuff, Declan, I want to try and illuminate one of the great St Thomas's

Community College mysteries. Why was Mr Catchpole on so many school trips? We had this theory that it was written into the school constitution. Or perhaps he was a train spotter, a closet cheese fanatic, a reincarnation of a First World War general or a frustrated tour guide – or maybe he was just unhappy at home. That afternoon at least, Mr Catchpole provided the answer himself.

'I suppose in a way the theatre was my first love,' he said, his voice booming up from the back of the coach. 'In fact, there was a time when I thought I might pursue it professionally. But I married very young of course, so that little dream fell by the . . .'

The journey to Brighton was the ultimate guilt trip. By the time we merged onto the dual carriageway, one simple question was burning a hole in my cranium.

What kind of a friend *was* I?

I think we both know the answer to that, Declan. And I had a horrible feeling that Ariel did too.

Everything I laid eyes on reminded me of you: the Coke can rolling in the aisle, the adjustable ventilator device under the luggage rack that we always fought over, that stain on the back of the seat, the people-carrier whose registration couldn't possibly have been DEC 1 – even the coach driver's moustache had a touch of the Declan Norris about it. But when I tried closing my eyes it got worse. I kept re-running the night of the crash, like it was on a permanent loop in the back of my head.

Whatever the camera angle, it didn't look good for me. And it didn't help matters that I could almost hear you doing your very own director's commentary: *'No, you're right; it looks pretty dodgy from where I'm lying too. No wonder you feel like crap.'*

By the time we got to the theatre, I was so freaked out it was a miracle I managed to find my way to the back of the royal circle. I buried my nose in Will's programme, doing everything in my power to ignore the fact that Ariel was sitting on the end of the row, spying on me.

'The play's the thing, eh?' said Will, turning his phone to silent and settling back in the plush velvet seat.

He couldn't have got it more wrong. Even the play made me feel guilty. When the girls started denouncing witches at the end of Act One, it was all I could do not to run screaming from the theatre. So I hung onto my seat, eyes tight shut, listening to the actors shouting at each another, like they always do in proper plays.

Perhaps I should have stayed there to the bitter end, because I still feel sick when I think about what happened next.

'OK, my friend,' said Will, as the lights went down at the start of the second half. 'Let's get out of here.'

He pushed his way to the end of the row. I followed blindly. Anything was better than another hour-and-a-half of Pulitzer Prize-winning drama.

'Where are you going?' whispered Ariel. 'You can't just leave.'

An irate pensioner turned and shushed, his hearing-aid squealing.

'Cheer up, Granddad,' said Will. 'You might be dead tomorrow.'

Ariel grabbed his arm. 'You'll never get away with it, you know.'

Down in the front row, Mr Catchpole was already engrossed in the courtroom scene, and Mrs Woolf had seized the opportunity to rest her eyes.

'Oh yeah, I forgot,' said Will, taking his arm back and heading for the door. 'Security is so hot at this school.'

Things got even more surreal when Ariel started begging. 'Will . . . *please*. Go on your own if you like, but leave Chris here with me. He looks terrible.'

'And whose fault is that?' said Will. 'What he needs is a bit of fun, not some dumb memory box.'

I had to escape from Ariel. The closer I got to her, the guiltier I became. Will stood beneath the exit sign, holding back the red curtain for me, like an expectant matador.

It was my only way out.

'Chris, wait,' hissed Ariel. 'You're in no fit state to —'

Freedom beckoned. We thundered down the cold stone staircase, the sense of elation momentarily numbing my feelings of hopelessness. Will flung open the fire doors at the bottom. An icy power-shower of torrential rain was waiting to greet us. 'I promised you some fun, didn't I, matey?' he said, hurriedly buttoning his trench coat. 'But I bet you weren't expecting a whole palace of it!'

Brighton may well be a cosmopolitan city with a thriving comedy scene, but on a stormy afternoon in December you'd do better to check out one of its numerous vegetarian restaurants or coffee outlets than wander the streets. But Will was a man in a hurry. I limped along behind him – down East Street, past a plethora of posh frock shops and over-priced soap emporiums until we arrived on the seafront. Half a decade later, I was forced to admit that Marvo the mime artist's walking against the wind routine wasn't nearly as terrible as I'd imagined. We clung to the pale green railings, watching waves the size of bungalows batter the shore.

'It's my favourite place in the whole world,' screamed Will, struggling to make himself heard above the screech of the seagulls and the roar of the sea.

My soggy school uniform was shrinking to fit me like a straitjacket. And as dusk fell, the pier lights twinkled invitingly above the turbulent waters. Will turned up his collar and sprinted towards them.

'Great, isn't it?' he said, licking his lips as he surveyed the pungent fast food stalls outside the entrance. 'No wonder they call it the palace of fun. If a guy can't have a good old laugh on Brighton Pier, he might as well chuck himself in the sea. Now, how about some doughnuts, my treat?'

I'll never eat doughnuts again as long as I live. Lips dripping with sugar, salt, and grease, I peered through the slits in the wooden decking at the sea below, trying not to puke.

'Go on, have another one,' said Will. 'You need to keep your strength up.'

The amusement arcade was a flashing cacophony of jangly music and explosions, but at least it was warm and dry. Will changed a ten-pound note at the kiosk and handed me a plastic cup full of coins. 'There you go, matey. What could be funner than stuffing twenty-pence-pieces into a slot machine?'

And this was supposed to make me happy? The bloke on the sound system might have been having a Wonderful Christmas Time, but I could barely find the energy to place a two pence bet on the Grand National game.

Will, on the other hand, was in his element. After he'd blown-up a few helicopters and decimated a squadron of cyborgs, he set about liberating cuddly toys from a glass container with a metal crane. 'Now you know where I spent last summer.' He smiled, handing me a yellow puppy with a big fluffy nose. 'My dad and Holly were playing happy families at the marina, so I got pretty good at this.'

Every horse I backed seemed to hobble in last.

'The curtain comes down in forty-five minutes,' said Will, rolling his last coin towards a waterfall of ten pence pieces, 'so we'd better get a move on. But, before we go, would you mind if we got a little memento?'

The Portrait to Anywhere photo booth was down by the air-hockey tables. 'After you,' he said, waving me inside. 'Don't worry, I've got plenty of spare change in my jacket.'

It felt more like the road to nowhere. I shuffled uncomfortably on the cold plastic seat.

Will squeezed in beside me, draping an arm across my shoulders and pulling closed the curtain. 'So where's it to be, then? Venice? The Pyramids? Tell you what, let's try Hollywood, shall we? OK, here comes the red light. Don't forget to smile now.'

Two flashes later we were waiting outside for our prints to drop. Will paced impatiently, knocking his knuckles together in time to 'Poker Face'.

'At last,' he said, grabbing the photos from the hole in the side and waving them in the air to dry. 'There you go, matey – one for you . . . and one for me. I'd put it in your pocket if I were you. We don't want it getting wet, do we?'

And there we were, standing in front of the Hollywood hills. But whilst Will looked like he'd just got the lead role in the latest blockbuster, I had the face of someone about to come to a nasty end in a soap.

'Come on,' said Will. 'Let's have one last look on deck. I love the rain, don't you?'

It's not surprising there weren't many punters about, just the occasional hoodie and a few middle-aged couples testing their new anoraks. Because if anything the storm was wilder now; the wind smacked you in the guts like a Darren Denyer pile driver and a fine sea-spray was sprinkling the deck.

Will marched purposefully onwards, sharing his philosophy with yours truly and the cloud-covered moon. 'Have you noticed how no one can say goodbye any more; how they're always desperate for you to "take care"?' He pointed at a sign. *It is dangerous and forbidden to jump, dive or swim from the pier.* 'Don't drop litter, don't feed the birds, always keep your shirt on in the Ocean Fish Bar. But you know what I say? I say, if you really want to be happy, you've got to be reckless!'

I wasn't sure I'd ever be happy again.

'Now we know where Ariel spends *her* summer holidays,' said Will, laughing uproariously at the tarot reader's Romany caravan. 'Maybe we should get our cards read.'

I didn't care about the future. In fact, I didn't care very much about anything. If I'd wanted full marks in GCSE English, I would probably have said that the storm inside my head was every bit as ferocious as the one raining down on me, but right at that moment, I didn't give a toss.

'I know I keep saying it,' said Will, grabbing my arm and steering me towards the thrill rides, 'but you've got to try and forget him – your friend Declan. I mean, let's face it, he's not coming back.'

And suddenly it hit me; suddenly I knew it was time to take matters into my own hands.

'Steady, matey; where's the fire?' said Will, as I pulled away from him and started running. 'Wait up, Christopher. Where are you —?'

I didn't *know* where I was going. All I knew was that Will was right. My only hope was to try and forget. But if I was ever to smother those devastating feelings of guilt, even for a few seconds, I needed to do something so completely reckless it would blow my mind.

At Horatio's Bar, I took a sharp left and made towards the deserted rifle range.

'Look, there's nothing down here,' said Will. 'I know this place like the back of my hand.'

He was wrong. Lurking in the shadows was the answer to all my prayers; a rusty metal gate secured with a padlock and chain. On the front was a red circle containing the faceless, silhouette of a man walking; beneath it the words *Strictly No Access*.

'See what I mean,' said Will. 'Talk about health and safety gone mad.'

I inched forward on the slippery decking, grabbing hold of the gate and forcing myself to look down. A rusty flight of steps descended into the shadows. In the summer they might have led to a landing stage for the speedboat. Out of season they simply disappeared into the angry sea.

Will peered over my shoulder into the churning void. 'Better not get too close, matey.'

I counted thirty-six steps exactly. They were arranged in groups of eleven, the twelfth, twenty-fourth and thirty-sixth steps consisting of a triple-sized metal grid. Except at the very bottom, where the grid had been removed, leaving only a gaping black hole.

'Wooooah,' squealed Will, staggering backwards as a colossal wave crashed against the bottom of the staircase making the whole pier shudder. 'Maybe we should be getting back.'

All I wanted was for the pain to stop.

'What are you doing?' said Will.

The distant moan of 'Lonely This Christmas' wafted up from the amusement arcade. I stepped up to the gate and clambered over.

'Look, I know I told you to be reckless, Christopher,' said Will, laughing nervously, 'but I didn't mean . . . *suicidal*.'

Arms splayed like a tightrope walker, I clung to the handrails, trying not to look down. Like I said,

Declan, what I did was totally dumb, but in my head, it made perfect sense. You know better than anyone how terrified I am of drowning. (It was my top, least favourite method of dying; yours was that being buried alive with a pregnant rat thing.) If a raging ocean couldn't take my mind off things, then nothing could. There was something else too. I had this crazy idea that if you were still watching me, it might show you how sorry I was.

'I think you've proved your point,' said Will. 'Now be careful when you turn round.'

But I wasn't done yet. If I didn't look down, I could go even further. To my left was the English Channel, to my right, the dark underbelly of the pier itself and the forest of barnacled pillars that held it above water. It had the effect of a giant amplifier, turning the roar of the ocean into a deafening symphony of the sea.

Eight . . . nine . . . ten steps I counted, until somehow I actually made it to the first metal grill. And that's when I threw up, hurling a sticky stream of spicy sausage pasta and doughnuts into the howling wind.

'Brilliant, matey, well done,' called Will, his fake laughter sounding suspiciously like desperation. 'But I think you'd better call it a day. If my dad finds out about this, he'll go mental.'

His hilarity receded even further when I started descending once more.

'I really don't think you should . . . look, *hurry up* . . . I can't wait much longer.'

The steps were rustier now. And every time a wave crashed against the bottom of the staircase it was a struggle to keep my balance.

And that's when I came to my senses. Or rather, that's when I realised I couldn't go any further and simply froze. Every muscle in my body refused point blank to cooperate, like one of those patients who wake up in the middle of an operation and find themselves completely paralysed.

Put it this way: it wasn't the best moment to discover that I really didn't want to die. If I died now, my secret would be swept away with me – and that didn't seem right somehow. On the other hand, it would have been the *perfect* moment to rediscover the power of speech. The experts insisted it was nothing physical, that it was all in my mind. So I summoned up what was left of my flagging strength and tried to scream for help.

Not a single syllable escaped my lips.

It hardly mattered anyway. Will was long gone. Only a maniac would be taking the air on a night like this. If I could turn my head a fraction I might *just* be able to . . .

Really bad move.

Because the next thing I knew I'd lost hold of the handrail, my legs buckled under me, and I was slithering backwards on my stomach towards a fathomless oblivion. Rudely awakened from my paralysis, I grabbed blindly for anything that could halt my clumsy descent. But my hands were frozen and the rusty metal was shrouded in a slippery mould, which made it practically impossible to get a grip. So it seemed like a miracle when I managed to jam my fingertips into the tiny holes on the underside of the step.

Until the wave came, that is. And then it just felt like a cruel way of prolonging the agony. Rising up out of blackness like an angry monster, it folded me in its salty arms and squeezed the life out of me, before falling away again – until the next time.

I don't know how it was with you, Declan, but they say that the moment before you die your whole life flashes in front of you. It wasn't like that for me. By rights I should have been enjoying my best bits, but all I could think about was how furious Mum would be when she discovered I'd bunked off in the middle of a performance, and that as double acts go, Norris and Hughes was probably the unluckiest duo in the South of England.

Every second I was haemorrhaging hope. I'd lost all feeling in my fingertips. There was a probably another wave coming at any minute, and even if I did manage to hold on again, it was highly unlikely that I'd ever muster the energy to start climbing. Only a traffic warden with superpowers could save me now.

* * *

'Come on,' said a voice. 'You can do this. I know you can. Let me help you.'

A gloved hand circled my wrist and starting pulling.

'Use your feet,' said the voice. 'And hurry up; there's another wave coming.'

This time it only tickled the soles of my shoes. I almost fainted with relief.

'Don't stop,' said the voice. 'We're only halfway there.'

The last remains of doughnut came back to haunt me. A sickly slither of sweetness shot from my mouth, like an angry bird.

'Do it for Declan,' she said, hauling me across the steaming pile of puke. 'Come on, come on. You can't give up now.'

Ariel must have been really strong after all that digging, because I could barely *feel* my feet, let alone use them. Back at the top, she grabbed my legs and bundled me over the gate like a sack of potatoes. I lay on the rain-swept decking wriggling my fingertips to make sure I was still alive.

Considering she'd just saved my life, Ariel sounded pretty furious. 'What were you *doing* down there? I told you Will would only . . .' She grabbed my arm and wrestled me to my feet. 'Come on, get up. We *have* to get back to the theatre. Do you think you can . . .?'

I was shivering so hard I could almost have drip-dried myself.

Her voice softened a little when she saw how terrible I looked. 'You can't go like that though. We need to get you warm first.'

She helped me back to the amusement arcade, positioning me beneath the heater at the main entrance, trying to ignore the suspicious glances of the old lady playing the Elvis fruit machine.

'Put this on,' she said, handing me her brown duffle coat.

It was way too small. Even so, I accepted it gratefully.

'Come on,' she said, leading me across to the air-hockey tables. 'I know somewhere you can rest for a bit.'

The Portrait to Anywhere booth still stank of Will's aftershave. At least it was private though. I would have hated anyone else to hear what happened next.

'You're still shaking,' she said, putting her arm around me and squeezing very tight. 'It's OK, Chris. You're safe now.'

It's funny how a simple act of kindness can make you feel so wretched. I didn't deserve it, you see. That's why I cried so bitterly. And why her whispered words of comfort only seemed to make things worse. 'That's right, let it all out, Chris . . . You're going to be fine, I promise. And you've got to believe me, none of this is your fault.'

Rob the Slob would probably be able to tell you if crying forever is a physical impossibility. Maybe you get dehydrated or something, because eventually, the tears dried up. Ariel waited until I'd wiped the last gobbet of sick off my chin before posing the inevitable question.

'I know you want to tell me, Chris. You've wanted to tell me for a while now. So how about I come straight out with it and ask you one more time? Why is that you can't talk about Declan?'

The moment I looked into Ariel's eyes, I knew I could resist her no longer.

'Because I killed him,' I said.

Ariel was no comedienne, but her double take was pitch-perfect.

'You can talk,' she whispered.

'Yes.'

She stared blankly into the hidden camera, as if she was posing for a passport photo. 'Hang on a minute. *What* did you just say?'

My new voice sounded different somehow; deeper and more confident. 'I said . . . because I killed him.'

'No, no, that can't be right . . . I mean, how could you have . . .?'

Ariel's truth drug irises demanded an explanation. Now that I'd blurted it out, I knew I'd have to tell her everything. 'You were right, something did happen. The afternoon before Ella's party, me and Declan had this massive argument.'

Out in the amusement arcade, the Elvis fruit machine vomited ten pence coins.

'We *never* argued. Well, only about stupid stuff like the silliest haircut in a sitcom or the worst British accent in a Hollywood movie.'

Ariel smiled knowingly. 'So what was it about?'

'It all started when . . .' But she didn't really need to know how it started, did she, Dec? It wasn't her fault that I'd picked up *The Self-Sufficiency Bible*. And besides, my dad says, '*It always starts with a girl*'. 'Declan said that . . . Declan said that . . .'

'Come on, Chris. What could Declan possibly have said that was so terrible?'

Perhaps I'd swallowed too much seawater. The words seemed to stick in my throat. 'He said that I . . . he said that I wasn't funny.'

At least I didn't have to explain to Ariel how serious it was. Everyone in Year Eleven knew that on planet Declan it was the worst insult in the universe. 'No . . . No . . . He couldn't have.'

'Well, he did,' I said, praying the old lady on the fruit machines hadn't been ear-wigging. 'And we weren't just best friends, we were a . . . well . . . a double act. All those Sunday afternoons we spent writing jokes or working on that dumb sitcom, and he didn't even think I was funny.'

'What, are you kidding?' said Ariel. 'It felt like every time I tried to start a serious conversation, he'd come out with the latest hilarious quotation from his best mate, Chris. I was quite jealous actually.'

'Sorry.'

'That's OK; some of them were quite funny.' The storm had somehow contrived to make Ariel's hair look neater. 'I still don't understand what you meant by —'

'You should have seen me. I was *so* angry with him. I just lost it completely. Some of the stuff I came out with was . . .' All those times I'd rehearsed it in my head, and I was still fluffing my lines. 'I told him to stuff his stupid double act; told him I never wanted to see him again.'

'Yes, but it still doesn't mean —'

'That's why I didn't go to Ella's party.'

'I know it sounds selfish,' said Ariel, 'but I remember being quite glad that you weren't there. It meant I had him to myself for a change.'

Now that I'd started, I needed to finish. 'Dec's parents were in Norwich for his sister's graduation.'

'Anna,' said Ariel. 'I met her at the funeral, she seemed . . . nice.'

'My dad was supposed to be giving both of us a lift home. Round about half-eleven, Dec started calling me.'

'We must have just left,' said Ariel. 'It was pouring with rain. Me and Mum got soaked on that tandem.'

'Three times I let him go through to voicemail. The fourth time I picked up. He was in a right old state.'

'What did he say?'

'He begged me to persuade my dad to come and collect him. It was turning a bit nasty in there. Dec had this feeling it was all going to kick off.'

'So what happened?' said Ariel.

'I said I couldn't give a stuff. I said maybe he should try phoning someone funny instead. And then . . . and then I told him to sod off and die.'

Ariel was uncharacteristically speechless. Surely I hadn't silenced her too?

'Don't you get it?' I said. 'If I hadn't been such a useless friend, he would never have got into that car in the first place. Dad would have turned up at the party with his stupid taxi-driver routine, and Declan would still be alive today. I killed him, Ariel. It's all my fault.'

She didn't speak for a very long time. Not for all four verses of 'All I Want for Christmas Is You'.

'It's not your fault, Chris. It was an accident, OK? How could you possibly have known the car was going to crash that night?'

'Yes, but I —'

'It's just life,' said Ariel. 'Bad stuff happens. Sometimes you're in the wrong place at the wrong time. Like poor Declan.

'And another thing,' Ariel went on, reaching around behind her neck and unclasping a delicate silver chain. 'If Declan didn't think you were funny, why did he give me this?' Hanging from the end was a silver memory stick.

'What is it?'

'It's your sitcom,' said Ariel. 'He told me to guard it with my life. Dec said *The Capped Crusader* was the funniest thing you'd ever written.' She pressed the precious memory stick into my hand. 'Here, you keep it. But don't go burning it this time!'

'How did you —?'

'It doesn't matter,' said Ariel. 'Just make sure you look after it, OK?'

And if you really want to know, Declan, I think I probably started crying again. No wonder Ariel was so keen for us to head back to the theatre.

I always thought that talking about it would make things worse. It was strange how I was feeling a tiny bit better already. I didn't quite believe her yet, but I could just about imagine that some time in the future, I'd probably be ready to move on.

The storm had nearly abated, and the audience was already spilling on to the pavement outside. Some of the St Thomas's kids looked even more traumatised than I was. But not one of them seemed half as relieved as Will Hunt when I limped across the road towards him.

'Thank goodness you're OK,' he said. 'Look, I'm really sorry, matey. I panicked, that's all. You know what it's like. I should never have —'

And he looked even more gobsmacked when I proceeded to tell half the audience *exactly* how I felt about him.

I'd been silenced long enough.

Eight Months
After The Crash

You always insisted on sitting through the final credits, just in case there were some spoof acknowledgements or a couple of funny out-takes. But I'm afraid there's not much more to say, Declan – except of course that I'm sorry, and I did tell you it was dumb.

Luckily, Mum was so delighted to hear my voice again that she didn't throw a wobbly when Mr Catchpole gave her a potted history of the Brighton trip. That came a few weeks later when I told her the whole story. But after she'd calmed down, she was actually really sympathetic. She told me that although your death was a tragic accident and I had *absolutely nothing* to feel guilty about, she'd always regretted that her last words to Granddad were 'Put your bloody teeth in,' so she kind of knew how I felt. Dad took it pretty well too.

And I couldn't help noticing that he stopped stressing about being made redundant after his 'quiet heart to heart' with Dominic and Holly about Will.

Will never came back to St Thomas's. He has a private tutor now. We saw him in town the other day with this bald guy who kept droning on about punctuation. This time it was Will's turn to give *me* the silent treatment. When I tried to say 'Hi,' he just flashed me the table lamp he was hiding in his inside pocket and walked straight past. Which reminds me, Mum insisted I take back all the stuff we nicked – apart from the toilet seat covers, which Pete had already used. Ariel could have made a brilliant shoplifter; she was way better than me at slipping everything back into place.

So come on, Declan, ask me who I'm taking to the prom next week? We've been going out for nearly a month now. There's so much about her that I didn't know – like how funny she is. In fact, she even helped me with the second episode of *The Capped Crusader*. As Kelly said herself, she was only sick once, so it was really unfair that puking up on the war graves trip in Year Seven was the only thing that people remembered her for.

Ariel's not going, of course. She still thinks school proms are a 'foul parody of a civil-servants' dinner dance'. But a whole load of us have hired a vintage bus and we're driving over to *Honesty Smallholdings* afterwards to watch the sunrise. We're good friends now, me and Ariel, just like you wanted, Declan. She's taught me so much, like how to recognise unhealthy chicken droppings, the difference between a dunnock and a whitethroat and that – crucial life-skill though it is – being funny isn't necessarily the most important thing in the world.

Losing you was the worst thing that ever happened to me. Don't laugh, Dec; I'm trying to be serious here. Like Dr Tennant said, we all deal with grief in our own way. The St Thomas's kids wanted to turn you into some kind of Facebook saint. I suppose my way of coping was to try and blank it all out completely. I see now how stupid that was. And just because we'd had an argument didn't mean we wouldn't have patched it up in the end. So, these days, I think about you a lot. I certainly don't need a memory box and it nearly always makes me smile. Because in my head, you see, you're still the same old Declan. I know you weren't perfect or anything (seriously, mate, get over yourself), but I really couldn't have wished for a better (yes, all right, *and* funnier) friend.

Now, before I go, there's something I should probably tell you. I wasn't sure if I should mention it, but Ariel says you would have been pleased for me, so here goes. The thing is, I've started working on a solo stand-up act. If we can't play the Edinburgh Festival together, I figure it's probably the next best thing. Don't worry, Declan, you'll always be my favourite co-writer. And every time I come up with some new material, I promise I won't forget to run it past you first.

Oh, by the way, you might be interested to know that the school council voted unanimously to plant a tree in your memory – which I thought was pretty ironic considering how you died. A few of us trooped down to the Demon Headmaster's conservation area for a low-key ceremony. Two clarinettists from the wind band played 'Shaddup You Face' and I told a – heavily censored – selection of your favourite jokes. Last, but not exactly least, Rob the Slob read a poem about dead people just being in the next room – and this time it kind of made sense.

Also by Simon Packham

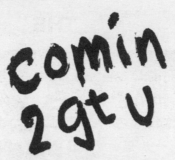

Sam Tennant has been brutally murdered in an online computer game. What's worse, it looks like his killers are out to get him in real life too. 'The Emperor' and 'Ollyg78' say they know him from school, and soon turn his classmates against him with their vindictive website.

With his father away, his mother preoccupied with a particularly difficult work case, and his dying granddad absorbed in some dark, wartime secrets of his own, Sam's only support comes from terminally shy Abby and Stephen the class nerd.

As the threats become more sinister, Sam faces a desperate struggle to identify his persecutors before things really get deadly.

'A great book for children and practically required reading for parents.' *The Bookbag*

'Packham gets across brilliantly feelings of isolation and fear . . . The action unfolds quickly, lucidly and logically – a cracking good read.' *Birmingham Post*

THE BEX FACTOR

She wants to be famous, now it's time to face reality!

When Bex gets an audition for *The Tingle Factor*, she begs geeky guitarist Matthew to accompany her, hoping he'll lift her performance.

But the judges want Matthew – not Bex!

Bex swallows her envy, and persuades a reluctant Matthew to take part by offering to help with his family. While Matthew gets swept up in the world of reality TV, it's Bex who has to deal with his sweet, affection-starved sister and his angry, disabled mother.

'Brilliantly drawn . . . compelling characters . . .
a very entertaining read.' *Chicklish*

FIFTY FIFTY

S. L. POWELL

Gil is on a collision course with his scientist father, and
when he meets Jude, a passionate animal rights activist,
things soon reach crisis point.

As Jude's plans become clear,
Gil is faced with a devastating dilemma
that goes right to the heart of his own identity.

'A riveting story.'
Irish Examiner

'A great, thought-provoking read for any young adult.'
Chicklish